AF447655

The One Who Kept the Light On

By

Tess Amara

Author's Note

This story is inspired by true events.

While names, certain details, and timelines have been changed to protect privacy, the heart of this story is real. The love is real. The loss is real. The faith that carried us through is real.

There were seasons in my life when I did not understand what God was doing. Seasons of illness, betrayal, grief, and heartbreak. Seasons when the prayers felt unanswered and the weight felt too heavy to carry.

But even then, God was present.

Not always in the way I expected.
Not always in the timing I would have chosen.
But present.

This book honors the quiet strength He gives when we have none left of our own. It is for the women who keep going when life falls apart. For the mothers and grandmothers who rise each day because love leaves no other choice.

If you are walking through loss or rebuilding after devastation, my prayer is that you find comfort here. That you are reminded you are not alone. That even in the darkest seasons, God is still holding the pieces.

Sometimes faith does not remove the storm.
Sometimes it simply gives us enough light to keep moving forward.

— Tess Amara

Chapter 1
The Quiet House

The house was too quiet now. Not the peaceful kind, but the kind that held echoes, reminding her of the voices that once filled the rooms.

Marie stood at the kitchen counter with her hands wrapped around a mug gone cold, listening to the low hum of the refrigerator. On the other side of the house, her granddaughters slept in rooms that once belonged to other versions of her life, her mother's room and the old guest room.

Some mornings she still expected to hear her mom's laughter drifting down the hallway, light and warm and unmistakable. And sometimes, when exhaustion softened the edges of reality, she thought she heard her daughter too, a soft footstep, a familiar presence brushing past her like air through an open window. Those moments tightened her chest more than anything else.

Her phone buzzed on the counter.

Aunt Carmella. Right on time.

"Hi, sweetheart," her aunt said, her voice steady and warm, one of the last living threads to the world Marie had lost.

Just like that, the silence shifted. It wasn't gone, but it felt easier to stand inside.

"How are the girls tonight?" her aunt asked.

"Tired," Marie said. "It's been a long week. They're settling in, but… you know."

There was a pause, the kind that exists only between people who understand one another without explanation.

"Your mom would be proud of you," her aunt said gently. "She always said you were the strong one."

Marie swallowed. Strength didn't feel like strength. It felt like survival, waking every morning and doing what needed to be done because there was no other choice.

Her gaze drifted to the photo of her daughter on the wall. The bright, determined smile that once lit up every room still seemed alive there.

"I miss her," Marie whispered, surprised by how raw the words sounded.

"I know, sweetheart," her aunt replied. "I miss her too. And your mama. Losing them both… it's too much for one heart."

Too much for one heart and yet she carried it anyway.

"But you're not alone," her aunt continued. "You've got those girls. And you've got me. We're still here."

Marie nodded, even though her aunt couldn't see her. "Thank you."

"Call me tomorrow," her aunt said. "I'll be here."

When the call ended, Marie set her phone down and looked again at her daughter's photograph.

"I'm trying," she whispered. "I'm trying for them."

The refrigerator hummed, and the house settled around her. For the first time in a long while, something inside her shifted. Not healing, not yet, but a quiet sense that she wasn't standing in the darkness alone.

Chapter 2
Morning Routines

Marie woke at 7:30, not because she felt rested, but because the dogs needed her. Florida light slipped through the blinds, soft and pale.

Tyson, her eleven-year-old Australian Shepherd and Golden Retriever mix, lifted his head the moment she moved. He didn't make a sound. He simply watched her, waiting for her to stand so he could follow. He never left her side.

"Come on, boy," she whispered, easing out of bed.

The house remained still as Marie stepped into the kitchen. Frances's door was half-closed; Duchess her Great Dane's shadow stretched beneath it. Frances was Marie's youngest granddaughter, the one the dog had claimed as her own from the moment she arrived.

Duchess slept on the girl's bed every night, curled protectively against her legs. She had been diagnosed with Addison's disease months ago, and while the medication had brought her weight back, it left her endlessly hungry. Still, she wouldn't move until Frances woke. That bond was unshakeable.

The dog had been one of her daughter's puppies from her last litter before she passed away. She had been returned broken, sick, and terrified. Somehow, the youngest granddaughter had become her safe place.

Marie took Tyson outside first. The two dogs simply didn't get along. He stayed close to her leg, as if the night swallow her if he didn't keep watch. The morning air was cool and gentle, the kind of Florida morning that made coffee taste better.

Inside, faint clicking came from the back bedroom. Sixteen-year-old Lynn was still awake, still playing on her tablet, her nights stretched long by ADHD and anxiety. She wouldn't sleep until the sun was fully up.

Marie stepped into Frances's room.

"Morning," Frances mumbled, her voice thick with sleep.

"Morning, sweetheart."

Frances blinked. "Ten more minutes?"

Marie brushed a strand of hair from her forehead. "Okay. But you have to get up when I call you."

Frances nodded, already drifting again. Duchess lowered her head back onto Frances's legs with a long sigh.

Marie stepped back into the living room. The house wasn't loud or busy, but it was full, of needs, routines, and the quiet, stubborn love that held them together.

Another morning. Another start.

And she carried it the way she carried everything else, quietly, steadily, one step at a time.

Later, when the bus had come and gone and the house settled again, her phone rang.

She didn't need to check the screen. It was her brother, Anthony.

Still in New York, alone now that his partner had passed and the partner's son had moved out. His world had grown smaller and heavier, and she could hear it in the way he said hello.

He talked about the apartment, the weather, the same small things he mentioned every day. But underneath was the strain he tried to hide, bills piling up, rent he struggled to cover, loneliness settling into the corners of his life.

Marie listened, her heart tight. She had helped him for as long as she could, stretching her own budget until it nearly snapped. But money was tight now, tighter than she liked to admit, and she could no longer carry him the way she once had.

Still, she felt the pull. The responsibility, the weight of being the one left.

"I know it is hard," she said gently. "But you are not alone. I am here. We will figure things out."

He sighed, the kind of sigh that carried years of exhaustion. He thanked her, even though she had not offered money, only presence. Sometimes that was all she had left to give.

After the call ended, the house slipped into late-morning quiet. Laundry hummed. Dishes clinked. The dogs watched and waited.

Life moved forward in small, steady pieces.

And grief lived in the quiet moments.

Three years had passed since her daughter died. Six months since her mom's passing.

People said time softened grief. For Marie, it hadn't. If anything, it had grown heavier, sharper than she ever expected. The missing did not fade; it deepened.

Some mornings the ache rose before she even realized she was thinking about them. Her daughter's laugh. Her mother's voice. The way both of them had filled the house with life, and how quiet it felt without them.

Grief didn't follow rules. It didn't fade on a schedule. It became part of her breath, part of the way she moved through the world.

Standing in the laundry room, folding warm clothes, Marie let her thoughts drift. The hum of the dryer and the quiet of the house had a way of opening old doors without warning, pulling her backward into moments she hadn't thought about in years.

One memory rose so clearly it felt like she was standing in her mom's bathroom at the old house in New York again, when Nina was about two or three years old.

Her mother had been watching Nina that day. Marie had come home, tired from work, expecting to find them in the living room. Instead, she heard crying from the bathroom. Not just one voice, but two.

She opened the door and stopped.

The walls were smeared with a thick, shiny coat of Vaseline, the jar sitting open on the counter like it had witnessed the whole disaster. Nina had apparently decided the bathroom needed a fresh paint job, and Vaseline was the perfect choice in her little mind.

Her mother was on the floor beside her, scrubbing the wall with a washcloth that only made the mess worse. Tears streamed down her face. Nina was crying too, not because she was in trouble, but because her grandmother was upset. The two of them sat there, covered in grease and frustration, clinging to each other as if the world had ended over a jar of ointment.

It had been a sight to see. A disaster at the time, but now it lived in Marie's memory with a warmth that hurt.

She had so many moments like that, so many pieces of their lives woven together. And now, for no reason at all, they came flooding in. Sometimes soft, sometimes sharp, sometimes so overwhelming she had to stop just to breathe.

The quiet of the laundry room held her there for a moment longer. The love. The loss. The ache that never really left.

Then she took a slow breath, steadying herself, and stepped back into the day waiting for her.

Chapter 3
The House Fully Wakes

Around this time, Marie heard the soft creak of the bedroom door opening. Her husband stepped out, moving slowly the way he always did in the morning. His short, military-style haircut looked exactly the same as it had for years, a habit he never let go of after his time in the Air Force.

He walked straight to the kitchen, Tyson lifting his head but staying on the sofa, knowing this part of the routine well. Marie watched as her husband filled his cup, added creamer, and leaned against the counter with his phone in hand.

The videos played loudly, the volume turned up because of the hearing loss in one ear. It was a familiar sound in the mornings, part of the rhythm of the house. He never liked to be bothered when he first woke up, and Marie respected that.

"Morning," she said softly as she passed through the kitchen.

"Morning," he replied, eyes still on his phone, voice rough from sleep.

That was enough. She left him to his coffee and his videos, giving him the quiet he needed. It was their rhythm; one they had settled into over the years.

After a while, once the coffee had done its work and the fog of sleep had lifted, he would come find her. He always did. He would sit down, set his phone aside, and that was when the real talking began.

"What's the plan for today?" he would ask, and together they would sort through it. Chores. Errands. Appointments. Whatever the girls needed. Whatever the house needed. Whatever life had thrown at them that week.

And then came the daily challenge: dinner.

It was the same conversation almost every day, trying to come up with something everyone would eat. Two girls with different tastes, her husband with his preferences, Marie trying to find something that didn't turn into a debate or a compromise.

"What do you want tonight?" he would ask.

"I don't know," she would say, because she truly didn't.

They went back and forth, tossing out ideas and rejecting them just as quickly. Some days they landed on something simple. Some days they gave up and made whatever was easiest. But they always tried.

It was ordinary, but it was theirs.

After finishing his coffee, her husband set his cup in the sink and headed toward the garage. His steps were slower than they used to be, careful in a way that showed the years of strain on his back. The injury he had suffered long ago still shaped his days, limiting what he could do, but he found ways to help where he could.

The garage was his space. Some mornings he tinkered with his motorcycle, adjusting something small or wiping it down even if it didn't need it. Other mornings he simply moved tools, checked things, kept his hands busy. It gave him a sense of purpose.

Marie had started to notice small shifts.

The sixteen-year-old slept deeper. Longer. Heavier. As if she were sinking into sleep instead of resting in it. Some mornings Marie slowed when she passed Lynn's room, listening for the fan, waiting for movement.

Too still sometimes.

Nothing she could point to. Nothing dramatic.

Just… different.

Tyson watched her more closely too, lifting his head whenever she moved, eyes tracking her with quiet awareness. The house was the same, but something inside it wasn't.

Later, the bedroom door creaked open and Lynn stepped into the living room, hair messy from sleep, moving on autopilot.

"Hey, sweetheart," Marie said gently.

Lynn gave a small nod and went to the fridge, grabbed a drink, let the cold air hit her face, then moved to the counter. Tyson went to her side, slow and steady, close enough to lean into.

Marie watched from across the room, the familiar ache settling into her chest.

"Did you sleep at all last night?" she asked softly.

Lynn shrugged. Quick. Automatic.

She sat on the couch beside the Tyson, leaning into his warmth as she checked her tablet. He settled beside her, calm and patient, as if he understood how fragile her mornings could be.

The house grew quiet again, but not the comforting kind. Lynn was awake, but something in her still felt far away.

The quiet stretched over the living room like a thin blanket. The tablet lit Lynn's face in soft, shifting light, and every now and then she reached down without looking, fingers moving through the dog's fur in absent circles. It was automatic. Familiar. Comfort that didn't need to be asked for.

Marie stayed in the kitchen, watching without letting it look like watching. The refrigerator hummed. The dryer clicked. A car passed outside. Ordinary sounds, normal sounds. But the room still felt thin around the edges.

"Do you want toast or something?" Marie asked finally, keeping her voice light.

Another small shrug.

"That's okay," Marie said softly. "I'll make some anyway."

She moved through the kitchen slowly, giving Lynn space to exist without pressure. Bread into the toaster. Butter on the counter. Coffee warming in the pot. Motions she could do without thinking.

The toast popped, loud in the quiet, and Marie flinched before she could stop herself.

She plated one slice, butter melting into the heat, and carried it to the coffee table, setting it down within reach.

"Just in case."

Lynn didn't look up, but a minute later she reached for it, took a small bite, and chewed slowly.

Marie let out a slow breath.

She rinsed a dish that didn't need rinsing and wiped a counter already clean, giving the moment room to stay ordinary. The garage door rattled softly as her husband moved something heavy, metal clinking against metal. The sound carried through the house like background music. Familiar. Safe.

Tyson shifted closer to Lynn, resting more of his weight against her leg. She didn't look down, but her fingers moved automatically, settling into his fur. The rhythm of it was slow, absent, comforting.

The silence lingered.

Marie watched from the kitchen sink; hands submerged in warm water long after the dish was clean.

Certain mornings felt like walking across ice.

You moved slow.

You didn't make sudden noise.

You listened for cracks you couldn't see.

Lynn finished half the toast and set it down. Not pushed away. Not forgotten. Just… paused.

That was something.

Marie dried her hands on a towel and leaned lightly against the counter.

"You've got online classes today, right?" she asked, casual, like she was asking about the weather.

A nod this time. Small. But clearer.

"Okay," Marie said. "We'll get set up after a bit."

Lynn's fingers moved faster on the tablet now. Not frantic. Just focused. The way she got when she was slipping into whatever world lived behind the screen.

Tyson lifted his head and looked at Marie.

Just for a second.

And something in that look tightened in her chest.

Like he knew she was counting the small wins. Out of bed before noon, answering with more than a shrug. Some days, that was everything.

Outside, the Florida sun climbed higher, pressing warmth against the windows. The house filled slowly with light, soft gold stretching across the floor, creeping toward the couch, toward Lynn, toward the dogs stretched around her like quiet sentries.

Marie pushed herself off the counter and moved toward the laundry room to switch the dryer, letting the normal sounds of the house keep moving.

In front of her, she heard the faintest sound.

Not words.

But not silence either.

A small hum. Low. Almost like Lynn didn't realize she was doing it.

Marie didn't turn around. She didn't react.

She simply let the sound linger in the air.

For the first time that morning, the house didn't feel like it was holding its breath.

It felt like it was waiting.

Chapter 4
Small Victories

Later that morning, her husband came back inside from the garage. He poured another cup of coffee, added creamer, and stirred it longer than necessary, the spoon tapping softly against the mug. Marie stayed at the sink, letting him have his quiet space the way she always did.

"Frances make the bus okay?" he asked.

"Yeah," Marie said. "She did."

He nodded and took a sip of coffee. After a moment, he asked, "You sleep any?"

"Some," she answered. It wasn't a lie, but it wasn't the full truth either. He understood that without needing more explanation.

"I'm going to run to the store later," he said. "We're low on milk."

"Okay."

They stood there for another second, the kitchen quieting around them.

"Dinner ideas?" he asked, already half-expecting the answer.

"Not yet," she said with the faintest smile.

"Figures."

There was no irritation in his voice, just routine. He finished his coffee, rinsed the cup, and set it carefully in the sink. Before heading back out, he paused with his hand resting on the counter.

"You good?" he asked quietly.

Marie dried her hands on a towel. "Yeah," she said. "I'm okay."

He gave a small nod and went back toward the garage, the door closing softly behind him.

Marie stood for a moment, listening to the familiar sounds of the house, the hum of the refrigerator, the washer shifting cycles, the faint tapping of Lynn's tablet from the living room. Then she grabbed a bottle of water from the fridge and carried it out.

"Drink some," she said casually, setting it on the coffee table within reach.

Lynn glanced at it and nodded. Marie didn't press. She moved to the chair across from the couch and sat down, close enough if she was needed, far enough not to crowd.

"You're going to do some schoolwork today?" she asked gently.

There was a pause before Lynn answered. "Yeah."

It wasn't loud, but it was clear.

"Okay," Marie said. "We'll get you logged in in a little bit."

Lynn shifted slightly, sitting a bit straighter. Tyson adjusted with her, resting more of his weight against her leg. Marie noticed the small change in posture, the way Lynn seemed just a little more present than she had been earlier.

Outside, the neighborhood carried on with its usual rhythm. A lawn mower started down the street. A car door slammed. Someone called out to a child in a yard nearby. Life continued, steady and unaware of the quiet negotiations happening inside this house.

Marie leaned back in the chair and let herself breathe for a moment. The room felt steadier now, not because anything dramatic had happened, but because the small pieces had begun to fall into place. Lynn had eaten half a slice of toast. She had answered a question. She had agreed to schoolwork. None of it would look like much to anyone else, but Marie knew better.

By early afternoon, the house had settled into a fragile calm. Lynn was still on the sofa, Tyson pressed against her side, her tablet resting on the cushion beside her. The pill Marie had left on the table was gone, the empty cup beside it a quiet sign that she had taken it without a fight.

Marie noticed it immediately, her chest easing just a little.

Later, she picked up the broom and began sweeping the floors in slow, even strokes. The sound was soft and rhythmic, something predictable in a day that always felt slightly fragile. She waited until Lynn's shoulders seemed looser before speaking again.

"Thank you for taking it," she said gently, not making a big deal of it.

Lynn's fingers paused briefly over the tablet screen. Not a full stop, just enough to show she had heard.

Marie didn't add anything else. She stepped back, giving her space, letting the moment stay light. Progress, in this house, was rarely loud. It happened in inches, in breaths, in moments most people would miss. Marie paid attention.

As Marie watched Lynn settle back into her screen and Tyson curl closer at her side, she felt the familiar weight in her chest, the quiet knowledge that nothing in her life had ever come easily. Every season of love had been earned through struggle. Every moment of stability had been fought for.

She hadn't always been this strong. She had learned it the hard way.

Chapter 5
The Shift

Long before Marie became the steady center of her family, before she learned how to hold everyone together, she had learned what it meant to be fragile.

Marie was fifteen when everything in her life shifted.

Before that, she had been an average teenager, going to school, hanging out with friends, laughing in hallways, and thinking more about weekend plans than anything serious. Her world was simple and predictable.

Then the nosebleeds started.

At first, they were just annoying. A towel pressed to her face. Her mom fussing. Both thinking it was nothing. But they kept happening, stronger each time, leaving her dizzy and pale. Eventually, her mom rushed her to the hospital, expecting a quick visit.

It wasn't.

What was supposed to be a short stay stretched into days, then weeks, then months.

The doctors ran test after test, their faces growing more concerned each day. Her red blood counts were high. Her platelets were dangerously low. No one could explain why.

Marie remembered lying in that hospital bed, staring at the ceiling tiles, listening to the machines beep steadily beside her. She remembered her mom's worried face, the way she tried to stay strong even when fear crept into her eyes.

When the diagnosis finally came, ITP, Immune Thrombocytopenic Purpura. Marie didn't understand the medical words, but she understood the seriousness in the room. She understood the way her mom held her hand tighter, and that something in her life had changed forever.

Surgery followed, and recovery moved slowly. Each step required effort. Each breath felt deliberate. Healing did not rush.

Eventually, she was able to come home.

But home didn't feel the same.

Marie expected to return to school and slip back into her old life, to sit with her friends at lunch and laugh about the things she had missed. Instead, she walked into hallways filled with whispers. Parents had warned their children to stay away from her, afraid she was contagious, afraid she was fragile, afraid she might die.

She wasn't dangerous, and she wasn't sick anymore, but fear rarely waits for facts.

Her friends drifted away one by one until she was left standing alone in the cafeteria, holding a tray she didn't want, pretending she didn't notice the empty seats around her.

Starting over at fifteen felt like being dropped into a world where everyone else already had a place and she didn't.

Still, she kept moving forward. She went to class, walked the halls, and came home to help her mom, quietly rebuilding herself one piece at a time. Without realizing it, that year taught her something she would carry for the rest of her life: how to survive when the world pulls away, how to keep going when she felt alone, and how to become the strong, steady woman others would one day rely on.

Chapter 6
Becoming a Mother

Around this time, Sophia met and eventually married Elmer, a gentleman she met at work. From the beginning, he was good to Sophia, to Marie, and to her brother Anthony. He had three children of his own, a son, Michael, who was the same age as Anthony, and two daughters, Ava and Lori.

Their families blended naturally. Everyone was rebuilding in their own way, and for a while, life felt steady again. Elmer's children came every weekend, the kids got along, and the house was full in a way that felt hopeful.

By the time Marie was old enough to date, she was finally starting to feel like herself again. She met Steve not long after, and for a while he felt like a fresh start. They dated for a few years, the kind of relationship that feels serious simply because it lasts longer than most do.

Marie trusted him. She trusted her best friend even more.

That was what made the betrayal cut so deeply.

Finding out they had been sleeping together behind her back shattered something inside her. It wasn't just losing a boyfriend. It was losing the girl she believed would stand beside her through anything. The heartbreak was sharp, humiliating, and lonely, and she struggled to understand how people she loved could hurt her so completely.

In the middle of that pain, she met someone new. A rebound. Someone who made her feel wanted when she felt invisible. She slept with him, trying to fill the emptiness Steve and her friend had left behind, never expecting it would change her life.

When she found out she was pregnant, her world tilted again.

Her parents were devastated, not angry, just heartbroken and overwhelmed. Still, they stood behind her. They supported her decision to keep the baby, and they supported her decision to marry the father, even though they had doubts.

After the wedding, Marie and her husband moved in with Sophia and Elmer. But it was Elmer who became the steady presence. He drove her to appointments when her husband didn't feel like going. He waited in hard plastic chairs in crowded offices. He carried folders, asked questions, remembered dates, and stayed engaged when others drifted away. Slowly, quietly, he became the person they all leaned on.

When the day finally came for the baby to be born, it was Elmer and her mom who got her to the hospital. They stayed with her. They paced the halls. They held her hand.

Her husband wasn't there. Not for the birth. Not afterward.

The pregnancy had been long and difficult. The delivery pushed Marie to her limits, and after her daughter was born, she went into shock. Her mom held the baby while nurses worked to stabilize her. Later, Marie named her little girl Nina.

Her husband was nowhere to be found.

After Nina was born, Marie tried to build a life with her husband. They moved into a small apartment, hopeful that having their own space would make things better. She told herself that every new beginning deserved a chance, that love and effort could fix what had already begun to crack.

But it didn't.

The verbal abuse came first. Sharp words. Put-downs disguised as jokes. Blame that always found its way back to her. Then the physical abuse followed. He began using drugs, disappearing for days, returning angry and unpredictable, bringing chaos into a home that was supposed to be safe.

Marie learned to listen for his footsteps. To read his moods. To keep Nina quiet when his temper flared. She lived in a constant state of watchfulness, never fully relaxed, never fully at ease.

She stayed longer than she should have. Longer than was safe.

Not because she was weak, but because she hoped.

She hoped he would change. She hoped Nina would soften him. She hoped that if she tried harder, loved better, stayed quieter, something would shift.

It didn't.

Before Nina was even a year old, Marie understood what she had been trying not to see. This life was not safe. And it never would be.

So she packed what she could. She held her daughter close. And she went back to the only place that had ever truly been home, her mother and Elmer's house.

She had a daughter now, and that little girl became the center of her world.

Back in her mother and Elmer's house, Marie began rebuilding from the ground up. She learned how to stretch every dollar, how to function on little sleep, how to balance work, childcare, and exhaustion without letting it show too much. She leaned on Sophia and Elmer more than she ever had before, grateful for their steady presence and the safety they offered when her own life had fallen apart.

Slowly and quietly, she became stronger, not louder, not harder, but stronger in the ways that mattered most: patience and resilience.

In the ability to keep showing up even when she was afraid.

She didn't think of it as courage at the time. She thought of it as survival.

It was laying the foundation for everything that would come next.

Chapter 7
Carrying On

The house felt different once Marie returned with Nina in her arms. Not quieter. Not heavier. Just rearranged.

Everything now revolved around feedings and naps and tiny cries that could rise without warning. Extra blankets were draped over the couch. Bottles lined the counter beside the sink. A bassinet sat near Sophia's bed for the nights when Marie was too tired to walk down the hallway. Every room seemed to bend itself around the needs of one small life.

Marie learned quickly that exhaustion had layers.

There was the tired that came from broken sleep, from waking every few hours and learning to function on little rest. And then there was the deeper tired that came from responsibility, from knowing that no matter how drained she felt, someone depended on her completely.

She learned how to warm bottles in the early morning light, how to rock Nina with one hand while folding laundry with the other. She learned which cries meant hunger and which meant discomfort. She learned that some nights nothing worked, and you simply stayed awake together until morning arrived.

She had no car. No steady job at first. No real plan for how everything would come together.

What she had was her family.

Elmer watched her closely in those early months. He never hovered and never interfered, but he noticed everything. He drove her to appointments without complaint and carried folders filled with paperwork she didn't yet know how to organize. He treated Nina as if she had always belonged there, as if she had always been part of the family.

Sophia carried the baby whenever Marie's arms trembled from fatigue. She reminded her gently that learning did not mean failing, and that needing help did not mean weakness. When Marie doubted herself, her mom quietly stepped in, not to take over, but to steady her.

Some nights, after Nina finally slept, Marie sat on the edge of her bed and stared into the dark, wondering how her life had changed so completely in such a short time. She missed being carefree. She missed being unafraid. She missed the version of herself who had once believed the future would unfold neatly.

But she never missed her daughter.

Not once.

Slowly, Marie found work. She saved what she could and learned how to balance schedules and bills and childcare. She learned how to plan meals around paydays and how to stretch groceries when money was tight. Each small success built confidence she hadn't known she was capable of carrying. It wasn't easy, and there were many days when she felt overwhelmed.

But she kept putting one foot in front of the other. Around that time, Ava came to live with them.

Elmer's middle daughter was still in high school, still trying to understand who she was and where she fit in a family that had been reshaped more than once. She and Marie grew close quickly, sharing late-night conversations and quiet understanding. They talked about school, relationships, worries, and dreams.

Ava met Paul not long after.

They were young and deeply devoted to each other. They adored Nina and treated her like something precious. They took her everywhere, to family gatherings, to stores, to sit on porches in the evening while they talked about their plans for the future.

One afternoon, Ava stepped out to run an errand, leaving Paul alone with Nina at his family's house.

When she returned, he stood in the middle of the room looking stunned, wipes scattered nearby, Nina freshly changed and perfectly content in his arms.

"Ava… she had an explosion," he said quietly. "I'm not kidding, it went everywhere. Up her back, all over her onesie. I didn't even know where to start. It was like a bomb exploded in her diaper."

They laughed about it for years.

It became one of those stories families carry forward, a reminder that even in rebuilding, there was room for humor and lightness.

Marie watched Ava and Paul and felt grateful. She was grateful that Nina had so many people who loved her, that her daughter was growing up surrounded by patience and kindness. Even on the hardest days, she knew she was not raising her child alone.

Life did not become easier overnight. There were still nights when Marie cried quietly into her pillow, mornings when she wondered how she would manage another day, and moments when fear whispered that she might fail, that she might not be strong enough for everything placed in her hands.

But each morning, she rose anyway. She fed her daughter. She went to work. She came home. She showed up.

She carried on, not because she was fearless, but because love demanded it. Because Nina needed her. Because her family believed in her. Because somewhere deep inside, Marie had learned that giving up was never an option.

Not long after, she met a man who was nothing like her first husband. He was steady, kind, and patient in a way she hadn't known before. They married, and for the first time in a long time, Marie felt like she had a chance at a real family. She learned shortly after that her ex-husband had gone to prison, a chapter she was relieved to close for good.

Her new husband had been married before and had a son, two years older than her daughter. The kids grew up together, sharing childhoods, routines, and the kind of bond that forms naturally when life brings two families together. When Marie's daughter turned seven, her husband adopted her, and from that moment on, they felt complete, a real family built from love and second chances.

For fifteen years, Marie poured herself into that marriage. They raised two teenagers, navigated school years, sports, arguments, laughter, and the everyday chaos of family life. She believed they were solid, that they would grow old together.

But marriages don't always break loudly. Sometimes they just wear down, piece by piece, until there's nothing left to hold on to.

After fifteen years, it fell apart.

Once again, Marie stood among the ruins of a life she had worked so hard to build.

But she didn't give in to it.

She gathered the pieces, the way she always had, and kept moving forward — not because it was easy, but because love and responsibility left her no other choice.

Chapter 8
Echoes of the Past

When Marie's daughter turned seventeen, life took a turn that felt painfully familiar. Nina was living with her boyfriend at the time when she announced she was pregnant. For Marie, it felt like watching her own past unfold again, the same fear, the same uncertainty, the same questions she had once asked herself.

Just like Marie had done years earlier, Nina left her boyfriend and moved in with Marie's mom. At the time, her mom was still grieving the loss of her husband, who had died of lung cancer at only fifty-four. The house had been unbearably quiet since then, heavy with absence and memory. But when Nina moved in, pregnant and scared, something shifted. The baby gave her mom a reason to get up in the morning, something to hold onto, something to live for.

Marie, meanwhile, was still trying to find her footing. She carried the weight of every decision she had ever made, every wrong turn, every moment she wished she could redo. She wanted more for herself. She wanted better.

So, she made a choice that would change everything.

She went back to school.

Accounting and business finance were two fields she had never imagined herself studying when she was younger. But she worked hard, pushed through doubt, and earned her degree. For the first time in a long time, she felt like she had built something solid, something she could stand on.

After graduation, Marie realized there was nothing left for her in New York, too many memories, too much pain, too many closed doors. So she packed up her life, and her mom and granddaughter moved with her to Florida.

It felt like a fresh start, a clean slate, a chance to breathe again.

By then, Nina was already in another relationship and planning to move out of state with him. Before she left, she asked Marie to care for Brooke until she was settled.

Marie didn't hesitate. She stepped into the role without question or complaint.

Starting over was something she understood well.

Florida felt like a fresh start from the beginning. Marie felt it the moment she stepped into the warm air and sunlight. Her mom felt it too. After losing her husband, she needed something new, something hopeful, something that reminded her she still had a life to live.

Having Brooke with them made the transition easier. That little girl brought laughter back into the house, filled the rooms with energy, and gave both Marie and her mom a renewed sense of purpose. They settled into Florida life, grateful for the sunshine, the slower pace, and the chance to breathe.

Chapter 9
A Place to Land Again

Years passed, and Brooke moved back and forth between her mom's home and Florida, always returning when she needed stability. During that time, Marie found work in an accounting office. It was steady, meaningful work, and it grounded her in ways she hadn't expected.

That was where she met Tom.

He was gentle and patient in a way that felt safe. They dated for several years, taking their time and letting the relationship grow naturally. Eventually, they married, building a quiet, dependable life together.

But while Marie was finding her footing, her daughter was losing hers.

Nina had been with her partner for seven years, and the relationship had slowly worn thin. Arguments became constant. Distance grew. Eventually, there was nothing left to hold them together. After they split, Nina learned she was pregnant again.

The news devastated her.

She was alone. Expecting a child. Her partner wanted nothing to do with the baby. She had no family nearby and no real support system.

Marie didn't hesitate.

She told Nina to come home. To come to Florida. To be with family. She reminded her that she didn't have to face this alone, that she had a place where she was loved and supported no matter what.

And Nina listened.

She packed up her life and came home.

Getting to Florida, however, was its own adventure.

She was pregnant with Lynn, caring for Brooke, and breeding chihuahuas at the time. When it was time to leave, she didn't just pack clothes and baby supplies. She packed her entire world.

Brooke climbed into the backseat with her toys.

The family's black lab squeezed in beside her.

A parrot in its cage was wedged between bags.

Ten chihuahuas filled carriers, laps, and blankets.

Nina's best friend and her father came along to help, and together they set off in a car and moving van that looked like a traveling pet circus.

It was chaos from the moment they left.

They stopped constantly, for bathrooms, dogs, restless kids, squawking birds, and tangled carriers. They ate on the road, reorganized animals, and tried to keep the chihuahuas from climbing over seats.

Even now, Nina's best friend still talks about that trip.

It was unforgettable.

And it was only the beginning.

Nina hadn't been in Florida long when everything changed again. She was settling into her apartment, building a routine, finally breathing after the move. Brooke was adjusting. The dogs were calm. Life was beginning to steady itself.

Then the contractions started.

Too early.

Too strong.

Too fast.

Marie and her mom rushed to her side and drove her to the hospital. Fear filled the car, but so did determination. They had done this before, not like this, not this early, but they knew how to hold each other up.

At the hospital, everything moved quickly. Doctors crowded the room. Machines beeped. Voices overlapped. Marie stood close, watching her daughter fight through pain she wasn't ready for.

Then came a tiny cry.

A tiny baby girl.

Lynn was so small and fragile, her skin almost translucent under the lights. Nurses worked quickly, checking her breathing, her temperature, her tiny limbs. Marie held her breath as she watched.

Lynn was placed in the NICU, surrounded by wires and warmers, fighting quietly. She stayed there for nearly a month, each day a mix of hope and fear.

And then, just in time for Christmas, she came home.

Nina carried her out wrapped in a soft blanket, the Florida sun warming her face. It felt like a miracle. A beginning. A promise that even in the hardest seasons, life finds a way forward.

Eventually, Nina gave up her breeding program. Two children were more than enough, and the demands of the dogs no longer fit the life she was building.

Letting it go wasn't easy.

It was necessary.

Chapter 10
When Life Turns Again

Not long after, life shifted again.

Nina met William almost by accident. He lived in the apartment directly behind hers, close enough that their paths were bound to cross sooner or later. What started as casual conversations, quick hellos, and neighborly check-ins slowly grew into something more. They began to date, finding comfort in each other's company, both of them carrying their own histories, their own wounds, and their own hopes for something better.

It was a quiet beginning, but a meaningful one, the kind that grows naturally when two people are in the right place at the right time.

While caring for her girls and building a new relationship, Nina was also searching for a job. When she finally got a call for an interview, she was excited and hopeful. She picked up the phone and called her grandmother.

"Grandmother, I have an interview at the mall," she said. "Can you watch the girls for me?"

"I can do better than that," her grandmother replied. "I'll come with you. While you're at the interview, I'll take the girls through the mall."

Plans were made, and the following week they headed out together.

But they never made it.

They were stopped at a light, waiting to turn when a car slammed into the back of theirs. The impact was so violent it threw their car across the road and into a fence.

Police and ambulances rushed to the scene. Everyone was shaken, frightened, and hurting. They were taken to the hospital.

Nina was conscious, but she had nerve damage to her face.

Her grandmother was covered in bruises from her waist down.

Brooke had bruises on her arms and legs.

But Lynn, only six months old, suffered the worst.

The force of the crash pushed her car seat from the back seat into the space between the driver and passenger seats. She was rushed to the children's hospital, where doctors discovered fluid on her brain. A shunt was placed to drain it, and she was admitted to the NICU, where she stayed for more than a month.

During that time, Marie and Nina stayed with her, refusing to leave her side.

William called often and came to visit whenever he could. He showed up not just for Nina, but for the girls as well. Marie noticed. She remembered thinking, "A man who doesn't just date a woman, but truly cares about her children too."

There were many sleepless nights and even more prayers.

But Lynn made a full recovery.

Not long after, Marie, still newly married, received news that stopped her cold.

Tom's mother had fallen and wasn't doing well. She had been taken to the hospital for a hip replacement, but while she was there, doctors discovered something far worse.

Cancer.

The shock settled deep in Marie's chest. It felt impossible that so much could be happening at once, but it was real, and it was happening fast.

Tom's mother was clear about what she wanted. She did not want to spend her remaining time in a hospital. She wanted to stay in her own home.

Marie didn't hesitate.

She looked at her husband and said, "Pack your bags. You're going to stay with your mom. I'll come straight after work on Fridays and stay until Sunday."

And that's exactly what she did.

For six months, Marie lived between two worlds. During the week, she worked, managed her home, and held everything together. Every Friday after work, she drove to her mother-in-law's house and stepped into the role of caregiver without complaint.

She did laundry, helped wash and set her hair, and sat beside her bed when the days felt long.

She talked when company was welcome and stayed quiet when silence was needed. She offered comfort in the ways that mattered most, through presence, patience, and love.

Tom wasn't alone in offering comfort.

He had brought their dog, Sadie, with him when he stayed with his mother. Since Marie worked all week, it made sense. Sadie adored Tom's mom. She would sit pressed against her side, listening as she talked in a soft, affectionate voice. In a strange way, Sadie seemed to understand, tilting her head, responding with quiet grumbles and gentle tail wags, as if she were talking back.

Every morning, Tom took Sadie outside to get the newspaper. With her tail wagging proudly, she would pick it up and trot straight to the bedroom, delivering it like it was the most important job in the world.

It became a small ritual, a bright spot in heavy days that always made them smile.

Tom stayed by his mother's side through it all.

He was with her when she passed.

Chapter 11
The Calm Before the Storm

For a long while, things finally seemed to settle.

Nina and William were adjusting into life with the girls, and then came news that surprised everyone: Nina was pregnant with baby number three. The couple was shocked but happy, and they began planning their future together with hope and excitement.

Frances, like Lynn, came early. She was tiny, fragile, and perfect, just like her sister had been. She, too, spent time in the NICU, but only for a short time. Soon enough, William and Nina were able to bring her home.

They planned a very small wedding, something simple and meaningful.

At the same time, Tom and Marie were moving forward with their own lives. They bought a big house with a pool, thrilled at the thought of their granddaughters splashing and laughing in the water. Life felt good, almost too good.

And then came another shock.

Tom was unpacking at the new house. Marie, her mom, and the grandkids were all there helping. From the bedroom, Tom called out, "I'm not feeling well."

It wasn't like him to complain.

Marie looked at him and said, "Let's go to the hospital and have you checked out. The girls all have colds; it's probably just an upper respiratory infection."

But when they arrived, everything changed in an instant.

They rushed Tom to the back. Marie still remembered the doctor leaning over him, saying, "Tom, Tom, you're having a heart attack."

Tom looked at Marie. The shock in her eyes was almost more than he could bear, but she tried not to show it. He knew anyway.

"Don't worry, babe. It's okay," he told her.

They took him straight to surgery, placed a stent, and later told Marie he had gotten there in time. There was no damage to his heart muscle. After a few days in the hospital, Tom was able to come home.

By then, William and Nina were married.

They built a life together, raising their girls, loving them fiercely, and doing the best they could.

They bought a home closer to Tom and Marie, and Nina decided to start breeding again, but this time with Great Danes. It was quite a change. She had gone from the smallest breed to one of the largest.

She brought her first Dane home, and when she was old enough Nina wasted no time having her bred. The puppies arrived, ten of them, one cuter than the next. She kept two and sold the rest, and that became the beginning of her new breeding program.

Her next litter was planned with the female she kept from the first litter. After many attempts and failures, Nina decided to add another female to the pack. With the new girl, success came on the very first try.

Litter number two was born. Twelve puppies.

The house suddenly felt much smaller with twelve puppies, three adult Danes, two kids, and Mom and Dad all under one roof.

It quickly became a full family effort to keep up with everything, the feedings, the cleaning, and the constant motion that came with a dozen growing Great Danes.

Soon enough, it was time for the puppies to go to their forever homes.

One by one, they left.

Until only two remained.

One that Nina simply had to keep, bringing the pack to five.

And one still waiting to be placed, lingering a little longer in the middle of their busy, crowded life.

Chapter 12
A New Kind of Closeness

They had barely caught their breath from everything that had come before when another change arrived. Marie's mom came to live with Tom and Marie. In order to help her keep her independence, they decided to build an in-law apartment on the property. That was when they met Tammy and Dave, the couple who would build the apartment and become part of their lives in a way that went far beyond construction.

Marie and her mom had so much fun picking out appliances and fixtures, choosing colors, and imagining how the space would feel once it was finished. It wasn't just a project; it was a new beginning for all of them. They were not only building a place for Mom. They were also building a close friendship with Tammy and Dave.

When the apartment was complete and Mom had moved in, things were looking up. Marie loved having her so close. Each morning, Mom would wake up, open her door, and walk across the way to Marie's patio, where Marie would be waiting with coffee and toast.

They spent every morning like this, sharing quiet moments, talking softly, or simply sitting together in the early light. It became their ritual, a small, steady calm they both cherished. Then the world changed.

COVID hit, and everything felt uncertain. The news was frightening, the rules kept shifting, and no one really knew what was safe anymore. But for Marie and her mom, it also brought something unexpected and gentle. They were already together, already in their own little world, already sharing their mornings on the patio. While everything outside felt chaotic, their routine stayed steady. In a strange way, it brought them even closer.

Marie became even more protective, watching over her mom, limiting visitors, and making sure she had everything she needed. Her mom had undergone quadruple bypass surgery, battled COPD and lung cancer, and lived with a pacemaker. She was on oxygen, and there was no way Marie was going to take any chances.

They cooked together, watched TV, talked about the past, and tried to make sense of the present. The world felt smaller and quieter, but their bond grew stronger in that stillness.

COVID affected so many lives. When schools finally reopened, it was only a matter of time before one or both of the girls tested positive. Sure enough, they did, and so did Nina and William.

With her compromised immune system, Nina quickly became worse and had to be transported by ambulance to the hospital.

The following day, William began having trouble breathing and had to go to the emergency room as well.

With the girls home alone, Marie got creative. She drove to their house with her laptop in hand and pulled into the driveway. She called the girls and had them FaceTime her on their tablets so she could keep an eye on them.

Nina's friends came by and left food and water at the door until William was able to return home.

Nina was still too sick to leave the hospital, and no one was allowed to visit.

By the grace of God, she made a full recovery and was finally able to return home.

During this time, Marie's mom and aunt stayed in close contact, just as they always had. But then the call came.

It was Marie's aunt, her voice thin and tired.

She told her they all had COVID. While one family member was getting better, another was getting sick. It moved through their house like a tornado, knocking each of them down in turn.

Months went by, and finally it looked like they had all made it through the worst of the pandemic.

For a while, it felt like life might be steady again.

For the first time in a long while, Marie allowed herself to believe they had made it through.

The worst seemed behind them.

The girls laughed more, Nina sounded stronger on the phone, and her mom sat on the patio with her coffee like she always had.

It wasn't perfect. Nothing ever was.

But it was livable.

And Marie was learning that sometimes, livable felt like peace.

She didn't know yet how fragile that peace was.

Chapter 13
The Beginning of the End

It started with something so small no one would ever think twice about. Nina stepped on a staple, just a tiny piece of metal, the kind you would normally brush off and forget. But for her, it became the beginning of something much bigger. The staple punctured her big toe, and within days the area grew red, swollen, and painful. At first, she tried to shrug it off, assuming it would heal on its own. It didn't.

The infection spread quickly, faster than anyone expected, and soon she could barely put weight on her foot. Being diabetic made everything harder. Healing wasn't simple anymore. What should have been a small injury turned into an open wound that refused to close. Weeks turned into months. She went to appointments, tried medications, soaked it, dressed it, elevated it, and did everything the doctors told her to do. Nothing worked. The infection kept returning, deeper each time, and the pain grew worse. Eventually, she found herself back in the hospital, exhausted from the fight and terrified of what they might say.

That was when the doctors told her the truth she had been dreading. They had to amputate her toe.

The surgery was done two days later, early in the morning before the sun had fully risen. Marie sat in the waiting room with her hands folded in her lap, staring at the same spot on the wall for hours, barely noticing the nurses passing by. When Nina was finally brought back to her room, she was pale and groggy, her voice slow and thick from medication. The bandages were wrapped neatly at the end of the bed, clean and careful, covering what had been taken.

At first, Nina barely seemed to notice them. It wasn't until later that afternoon, when she shifted suddenly, that she frowned and looked down. "Mom," she said quietly, "it's burning."

Marie stood up immediately, thinking something had gone wrong. The nurse came in calmly and explained that it was phantom pain, that sometimes after an amputation, the nerves still sent signals to the brain. The body hadn't caught up yet. Nina shook her head, confused. "But it's there. I can feel it."

"I know," Marie said softly.

And that was the hardest part, watching her daughter reach down to rub a place that was no longer there, watching her wince at pain that couldn't be fixed or explained away.

That night it happened again. Nina gripped the rails of the bed, eyes squeezed shut. "It feels like someone's crushing it," she whispered through clenched teeth. The nurse adjusted her medication. The monitor beeped steadily. The hallway lights dimmed. Marie stayed in the chair beside her, watching not just the pain, but the way Nina tried to pretend it wasn't serious.

"It'll heal," Nina said later, brushing it off. "It's just a toe. I'll adjust."

Marie nodded, though something in her chest tightened. She had heard the warnings. She had seen the numbers. She knew this hadn't come out of nowhere.

One afternoon, when the girls had stepped out with William, Marie leaned closer to the bed. "Nina," she said gently, "you have to start taking this more seriously. You can't keep pushing it aside."

Nina sighed. "Mom, I'm fine. I'll do better. I promise."

Marie wanted to believe her. She had learned that promises were easy when you didn't yet understand the cost.

The phantom pain came and went for days. Sometimes Nina laughed and joked like nothing had happened. Other times she lay silent, staring at the ceiling, exhausted from fighting something she couldn't see. When she was finally discharged, they told her recovery would take time, and they were right. Losing the toe changed the way she walked, the way she balanced, the way she moved through her day. Every step reminded her of what she had been through and what she was still fighting.

The surgery was supposed to be the turning point; the moment things finally started to get better. But recovery wasn't simple. Diabetes had already taken so much, and this infection had drained what little strength she had left. She tried to stay strong for the girls, for William, for her family. That was who she was. Tough. Stubborn. Determined not to let anything slow her down.

But her body was tired.

The wound healed slowly and painfully. Some days she seemed like herself again, laughing with the girls, trying to keep up with the chaos of the house. Other days she could barely get out of bed. The pain medication made her groggy. The antibiotics made her sick. The constant appointments wore her down. Still, she pushed through. She always did. But for the first time, the cracks were visible, the exhaustion in her eyes, the way she gasped when she thought no one was looking, the quiet moments when she sat alone trying to catch her breath.

This was the beginning of a long, difficult road. None of them knew it then, not fully. They kept hoping she would turn a corner, that the worst was behind her. But something had shifted. Little by little, her health began to slip. Fibromyalgia. Neuropathy. Each diagnosis added another layer of pain to a body already fighting too hard.

She got sick more often. Some days she could barely get out of bed. Other days she pushed herself anyway, even when simple things, walking to the kitchen, getting dressed, cleaning up after the dogs, left her breathless. Her energy faded first, then her appetite, then her strength. She lost weight without trying. She slept more. She moved slower. She laughed less. The sparkle in her eyes dimmed, replaced by a tiredness she could no longer hide.

Doctor visits became more frequent. Medications increased. She told them about the chest pain, the shortness of breath, the feeling that something wasn't right. They said it was anxiety. More medication. When that didn't help, they said it was asthma. An inhaler. Nothing helped.

Marie could hear it in her voice, the frustration, the fear, the exhaustion she tried so hard to hide. The girls noticed too. Children always know. And through it all, Nina kept going. She kept fighting, showing up for her family even as her body failed. But the truth was undeniable. This was the beginning of her decline, a slow, steady unraveling no one could stop.

Her symptoms worsened. The chest pain never left. The shortness of breath became constant. Some days she couldn't walk from the bedroom to the living room without stopping. She tried to pretend it was just another bad day, but Marie knew better. The inhaler didn't help. The anxiety medication didn't help. Nothing helped. Her body was failing her, piece by piece.

Some nights, Nina would call crying, saying she didn't feel right, that something was wrong, that she couldn't explain it but she knew her own body. Marie stayed on the phone with her, talking her through it, listening to her breathe, staying until she felt calm enough to sleep. But deep down, Marie knew, this was more than anxiety, more than asthma, more than exhaustion. Something was being missed.

And then came the day everything changed.

A morning like any other. Ordinary. Unremarkable. Until it wasn't.

The phone rang. Nina wasn't breathing. The ambulance was on the way. William was doing CPR. The girls were terrified. Marie rushed to the hospital, praying the whole way, begging God not to take her child.

When she arrived, their faces told her everything before their words did. They revived her, but her heartbeat was weak. They fought for her, worked on her, did everything they could. A ninety-percent blockage. A stent. The ICU. Words that barely made sense. Marie stayed by her side all night, holding her hand, whispering, begging her to wake up. She was only thirty-nine, too young, too needed, too loved.

By morning, she was failing. The staff told Marie it was time to call the family. No mother should ever hear those words. The family gathered. The girls stood by the bed. Marie's mom held Nina's hand. Everyone cried. Everyone broke. They made the impossible choice. The machines were unplugged. Within minutes, she was gone.

The world changed.

Some moments divide life into before and after. This was one of them.

Nina's passing left a silence that settled into every corner of the family. Marie carried that day with her, the phone call, the drive, the ICU, the goodbye. She replayed it over and over, trying to understand something that would never make sense. A mother isn't meant to bury her child. A grandmother isn't meant to watch her granddaughters lose their mother. A family isn't meant to break like this.

But somehow, they kept going. Not because the pain faded, but because love demanded it. The girls needed her. So, Marie kept moving forward, carrying Nina's memory with her every step. This was the moment that reshaped their lives, their routines, their hearts, their future. And though nothing would ever be the same, the love they shared with Nina would carry them forward.

Chapter 14
After the Storm

In the days that followed, everything felt unreal, as if the world had gone quiet in a way that didn't make sense. The girls stayed close to Marie, clinging to her, watching her every move, as if she were the only solid thing left in a world that had suddenly tilted.

William was shattered. Grief hit him in waves so heavy he could barely stand under them. He tried to be strong for the girls, but losing Nina broke something inside him. They had built a life together, raised their children together, survived so many storms side by side. Now he was left with a silence he didn't know how to live with. Every room reminded him of her, every sound, every smell, every empty space.

Marie saw it in his eyes, the way he moved through the days as if he was underwater, the way he tried to hold himself together but kept falling apart. She knew he loved his daughters, but she also knew he was drowning in grief too deep to navigate while trying to raise two little girls who were grieving.

And that was how the girls came to live with Tom and Marie. Not because William didn't love them, but because he was broken. Marie stepped in the way she always did, with love, strength, and the quiet determination that had carried her through every hard moment of her life. She opened her home, her arms, her heart, and the girls walked into a new chapter they never asked for but desperately needed.

But before any of that could happen, Marie had to do something she would remember for the rest of her life. She had to make the calls, the dreaded calls no mother should ever have to make. Calling her family, her siblings, her closest friends, saying the words out loud that didn't feel real. Each call broke her a little more. Each voice on the other end cried with her, asked the same questions she had no answers for, shared the same disbelief. She held herself together long enough to get through them. When the last call was made, she sat alone in the quiet of her living room, the weight of it all pressing down on her.

Her daughter was gone.

Her granddaughters needed her.

Somehow, she had to find the strength to carry them all.

That first night with the girls was one Marie would never forget. They arrived with small bags, tired eyes, and a kind of silence that didn't belong on children. They didn't run through the house or ask questions or explore. They stayed close, hovering near Marie and her mom as if they were the only steady things left in a world that had suddenly come apart.

Tom tried to make things feel normal, turning on the porch light, letting the dog out, asking if anyone was hungry, but the house felt different, heavier, as if it knew something had shifted. Even Tyson sensed it. He stayed close to the girls, nudging their hands, resting his head on their laps, offering the kind of comfort only animals know how to give.

Marie helped the girls settle in. She laid out blankets, fluffed pillows, turned on nightlights, anything that might make the unfamiliar feel a little less frightening. They changed quietly, moving slowly, as if every motion took effort. When it was time for bed, they didn't want to be alone. They asked Marie if she would sleep with them, and she did.

They didn't talk much. They didn't cry. They just lay there, eyes open, staring at the ceiling, trying to understand a world that no longer made sense. Marie stayed until their breathing softened, until their bodies finally gave in to exhaustion. Even then, she didn't leave right away. She watched them sleep, her heart breaking for everything they had lost, for everything they would have to learn to live without.

That night, the house was quiet, not the peaceful kind, but the kind that settles into the walls after a tragedy, the kind that makes every sound feel louder, every shadow feel heavier. Marie walked through the rooms, turning off lights, checking locks, doing the small routines that kept her grounded. But nothing felt the same. Grief had moved in with them. It sat in the corners, lingered in the hallways, pressed against her chest. Every room held a memory of Nina. Every silence reminded her of the calls she had made, the voices she had heard break on the other end of the line.

And yet, even in that heaviness, there was purpose. The girls were here. They needed her. They needed stability, love, safety, all the things Marie knew how to give, even when her own heart was shattered.

That first night was the beginning of a new life for all of them. Not a life they chose. Not a life they were ready for. But a life they would learn to navigate together, one day at a time.

The next few days passed in a blur, the kind that comes when grief is still fresh and every hour feels heavier than the last. There were decisions to make, papers to sign, people to call. Marie moved through it all on autopilot, funeral homes, service times, choosing photos, writing an obituary. Each task felt like another reminder that Nina was really gone.

Her ex-husband and his wife, along with her cousin and Nina's brother, came over to help with the arrangements. The girls sat nearby, watching quietly, their eyes still swollen from crying. Every so often, one of them would drift over to Marie's mom, leaning into her for comfort. She would wrap an arm around them, hold them close, then return to helping make decisions.

William tried. He showed up with red eyes and shaking hands, wanting to help, wanting to be part of it, but the weight of it all would pull him under again. Marie never judged him. She knew he loved Nina deeply. She knew this loss had shattered him. But she also knew the girls needed stability, and right now, he did not have any to give.

Family members called constantly, each conversation reopening the wound. Marie repeated the same words over and over, her voice steady even when her heart was not. Some calls ended in silence, others in sobs, all of them taking a piece of her strength. When the last call was done each day, she would sit quietly for a moment, letting the stillness settle around her, gathering herself before the girls needed her again.

The house felt different in those days, heavier, quieter, as if it understood the grief that had moved in. Even the dog seemed to know. He followed Marie from room to room, stayed close to the girls, offering comfort in the only way he could.

And in the middle of it all, Marie kept going. Because that was what she had always done. And now, more than ever, it was what her family needed.

Chapter 15
When the Caregiving Returned

Through it all, life did not pause. Meals still had to be made. Clothes washed and folded. The girls still needed reassurance, routine, and the quiet promise of safety that lived in ordinary days. Marie and Tom gave them that as best they could, even when their own hearts felt heavy and slow, as if they were moving through water while holding more than anyone should have to carry.

And just as they were beginning to find a fragile rhythm inside the grief, something thin but steady enough to stand on, another shift was coming. One that would change the house all over again.

It was time for Marie's mom to move into the main house.

At first, it was little things, the kind you brushed away because you didn't want to believe they meant anything. Her mom seemed more tired in the mornings, moving slower, as if each step had to be thought through before it happened. It took her longer to settle into her chair. Some days she didn't finish her toast, leaving the last few bites cooling on the plate. Other days she drifted somewhere inside her thoughts, staring past the room before gently returning, as though she had taken a trip no one else could see.

Marie noticed. Of course she did. She knew her mother in the way only daughters who have spent a lifetime watching know. But love has a way of softening fear, reshaping worry into something easier to hold. Maybe she's just tired. Maybe she didn't sleep well. Maybe tomorrow will be better.

Still, the changes kept coming, small, steady, unwilling to be ignored.

Her mom began forgetting little things: where she put her glasses, whether she had taken her morning pills, what day it was. One morning, Marie stood in the kitchen listening to the soft rattle of the pill bottle in her mother's hands. The sound went on too long, longer than it should have. When her mom finally looked up and smiled, waving it away as "old age," Marie smiled back, the kind of smile you give when you aren't ready to ask the question forming in your chest.

She didn't say anything. Not yet.

Instead, she began making small adjustments, quietly and carefully, as though doing them gently might keep them from meaning more than they did. She tightened the routines she already carried. She handled her mom's medications herself, sorting them carefully, double-checking doses, keeping track of the time without making it obvious.

As the changes deepened, those adjustments became something else, the kind you make when you are trying to stay one step ahead of something you are not ready to name.

She installed a small alarm near her mother's bed, one that would sound softly in Marie's room if her mom tried to get up during the night. Even thinking about it felt like crossing an invisible line.

Evenings became harder. As daylight faded, something inside her mother seemed to fade with it. She grew restless, unsettled, sometimes confused about where she was or why the house felt unfamiliar. Some nights she wandered slowly through the rooms, opening doors, moving as if she were searching for something she could almost remember but never quite reach.

Marie never named it. Not out loud. Not even fully in her own mind. Instead, she walked beside her, redirecting gently, speaking in soft, steady tones, guiding her back to bed the way she had once guided sleepy children under blankets. Only this time, her chest ached with a weight she couldn't put down.

During this time, Marie's aunt, her mom's oldest sister, became an even stronger presence. The two sisters had always been close, speaking nearly every day. They were the only two of the five girls who had built their lives in the States, while the others remained in Italy. Losing their youngest sister years earlier had shaken something loose in the family, a grief that never fully left, only settled quietly into the background of everything.

Her aunt called often, checking on her sister, checking on Marie, checking on the girls. Sometimes they spoke on the phone. Other times they used FaceTime so the sisters could study each other's faces, searching for things they did not want to say out loud. Even from a distance, her aunt could sense the shift.

"Marie, keep an eye on her."

"She looks tired today."

"Call me later and tell me how she is."

Those conversations became a lifeline; a thin but unbreakable thread stretched across miles and time zones. Two sisters who had survived war, immigration, motherhood, and loss now stood at the edge of something slow, quiet, and deeply unfair. Something neither of them wanted to name.

Marie held onto those calls even as she felt herself bracing against a future she could already sense approaching.

Sophia had always been a strong woman; the kind whose presence filled a room without needing to raise her voice. She was the third of five sisters, born in a small town in Italy where family was everything and life felt both simple and impossibly complicated. Her closest bond had always been with Carmella. They grew up side by side, sharing secrets, chores, dreams, and a connection time never loosened.

Life had not been easy for the five girls. They learned early how to work, how to endure, how to lean on one another when the world shifted beneath their feet. Those lessons shaped them. Both sisters eventually built lives in America. They married, raised children, and, almost amusingly, both became hairdressers. Each owned her own business. Each was known not only for skill, but for warmth, for the way people felt safe sitting in their chairs.

As Sophia began to slow, Carmella saw it too. Even through a screen, she noticed.

"Marie, keep an eye on her."

"She looks tired today."

"Call me later."

Miles away, she was still standing guard.

Sophia had lived a full, complicated, beautiful life. She had loved deeply, worked endlessly, built homes out of whatever life handed her, held her family together through storms most people never saw. And now, as she moved into the main house, Marie felt the shift settle into her bones.

It was her turn to carry her mother.

Her turn to be strong.

Her turn to return the love that had shaped her.

And love, she was learning, did not always look like grand moments or spoken promises. Sometimes it looked like listening in the dark.

As the weeks passed, the nights began to blur together. One folded quietly into the next. Sleep came in fragments, broken by alarms and soft footsteps, by confusion and whispered apologies, by the awareness that Marie could never fully rest anymore.

And still, life moved forward.

Coffee brewed every morning. The girls needed rides, reminders, reassurance. The house stayed full of ordinary noise and movement, but beneath it all was something fragile that Marie carried everywhere, a sense that if she looked at it too closely, it might break.

She found herself watching more, listening more, holding onto small things she had once taken for granted, the way her mom hummed while folding laundry, the way she reached for Marie's hand without thinking, the way she smiled when she recognized her, even on the harder days.

She memorized those moments without meaning to, as if some part of her already knew they would not last forever.

She did not talk about that fear. Not with Tom. Not with the girls. Not even fully with herself.

Instead, she kept moving forward.

At night, when the house finally grew quiet and the alarm sat waiting beside her bed, Marie lay awake longer than she needed to, listening for sounds that might never come and worrying about the ones that eventually would.

In those hours between sleep and waking, she felt the truth settling deeper into her bones.

Life was changing.

This time, there would be no stopping it.

Chapter 16
The Final Care

Marie had thought bringing in hospice would be a relief. She believed it would be the next step, a way to share the weight she could no longer carry alone. She imagined nurses arriving with quiet confidence, a steady presence in the house, someone who would guide her through the final days and make the long, silent hours feel less like a countdown.

But hospice was not what she expected.

The medications were changed and adjusted to keep her mom comfortable, and when Sophia stopped waking, stopped eating, and drifted further into sleep, it became Marie's responsibility to administer the very doses meant to ease her final hours. She had not imagined that part. She had pictured herself sitting beside her mother while someone else handled the details. She had imagined guidance, reassurance, a hand on her shoulder when the weight pressed too hard.

Instead, it was hers, fully and completely.

Tammy came to help, moving beside her through the dim rooms, whispering reminders, steadying moments that might have otherwise shattered her. Together, they cared for Sophia in those last days and nights, every touch and every careful adjustment becoming an act of love neither of them would ever forget.

Marie found herself listening more than she spoke, watching more than she moved. She measured time in small signs now, a twitch of a finger, a breath that came a little too quickly, the way her mother's hand curled or relaxed. She learned to notice changes so subtle they almost seemed imagined, leaning closer to be sure she was seeing them clearly.

Through it all, the girls still needed her.

She continued making meals, answering questions, offering comfort, even as part of her remained anchored beside her mother's bed. Somewhere in the middle of exhaustion and grief, Marie understood something she had never fully grasped before, that love is often measured not in grand gestures, but in quiet endurance, in staying present when your heart feels as though it is breaking with every passing hour.

During that time, the phone rarely stopped ringing.

Family members called constantly, their voices filled with concern and the quiet ache of knowing the end was close. Sophia's sister would FaceTime, leaning close to the screen, speaking softly, urging her to open her eyes, to respond, to know she was surrounded by love. Every word carried a lifetime of devotion.

Her son called every day, sometimes more than once, asking small questions that sounded ordinary but were weighted with fear. Her sisters in Italy called too, their voices traveling across oceans, trembling with distance and devotion. Messages poured in from nieces, nephews, and stepchildren, all worried that Sophia was slipping away too quietly, too quickly.

Marie held every call carefully. She answered gently. She updated everyone. She carried their worry alongside her own. Even when the house was physically quiet, it seemed filled with voices, with love stretching across miles, surrounding Sophia in ways no one could see.

Days and nights blurred together.

Marie moved through the house quietly, every step measured, every sound noted. The soft rasp of her mom's breathing, the faint shift of a hand, the flutter of an eyelid, these became the markers of time. She stayed close, hands ready, heart steady but breaking, prepared to respond to anything her mother might need.

Sometimes she leaned close just to feel the warmth of her skin, to reassure herself that Sophia was still here, still breathing, still part of the world she had built. There were no conversations left to have, no stories to share, only silence, broken occasionally by a murmur, the steady hum of the oxygen machine, and distant sounds of life continuing elsewhere in the house.

Administering the medication became one of the heaviest parts.

Each dose was meant to bring comfort, to ease pain, to guide Sophia gently through something Marie could not follow. But every time she gave it, she felt the weight of responsibility press deeper into her chest. It was a boundary she had never imagined crossing, and once crossed, she could not step back from it.

Tammy remained close, offering quiet guidance and steady hands when Marie's own began to tremble. There were no words that made it easier, no instructions that soothed the heart. They were simply there, together, doing the best they could.

Sleep came in fragments. Morning arrived too soon. And still, life moved forward.

Coffee brewed. The girls needed lunches. The house continued its rhythm, though every sound felt amplified and every shadow stretched longer than before. Marie felt the strain settle into her shoulders, her neck, her chest, in ways that never fully released.

She thought often of her mother's hands, of how Sophia had held her when she was small, of how love had always been given freely and without hesitation. Now it was her turn to return it, fully and without holding anything back.

As the hours grew thinner, Marie's attention sharpened until it felt almost unbearable. Every breath mattered. Every flutter of movement became monumental. She hovered close, her heart held tightly in check as grief and devotion moved through her at the same time.

Then, in the quietest hour, everything shifted.

Sophia's breathing slowed. The gentle rise and fall of her chest became uneven. A finger twitched once, and then lay still. Marie held her mother's hand, feeling the last warmth fade, listening to the steady hum of the oxygen machine and the distant sounds of life in other rooms.

And she wept.

Tammy moved closer, resting steady hands on her back. They shared tears in silence, the weight of presence enough where words could not reach. Marie whispered her mother's name and repeated the small phrases of comfort she had spoken for years, even though she knew no answer would come.

She felt the fullness of a lifetime pass through her in those moments, a quiet acknowledgment that Sophia's journey was ending and that it had been her privilege, painful and sacred, to walk beside her until the final breath.

Life would continue. The girls would still need her. The house would go on. But something essential had shifted forever.

Marie held her mother close a little longer, memorizing the shape of her, the warmth, the presence that had filled her life. Then she whispered the words she had been carrying through every long night:

"I love you so much. It's okay to go. I will be okay. Nina is waiting for you with all our loved ones."

When it was over, the house felt different.

The oxygen machine was silent. The rooms held only echoes. Marie sat beside the bed for a long time, her hand resting where her mother had been, letting herself breathe and feel and cry without restraint. Outside, sunlight moved slowly across the windows, soft and forgiving.

For the first time in days, she was simply a daughter who had loved fully, a witness to a life that had ended, and a heart that would carry it forever.

Chapter 17
After the Silence

The house felt impossibly still. Every corner, every shadow, every familiar sound carried an absence that pressed against Marie's chest. She moved through the rooms slowly, almost afraid to disturb the quiet, as if the mere act of living might shatter what remained of her mom's presence. The oxygen machine was gone. The bed, once alive with subtle breaths and tiny movements, now held only the memory of a life that had filled it so completely. Marie ran her hand over the covers, over the space where her mom had lain, and felt the hollowness, the weight of what could never be replaced.

The girls were quiet, each processing loss in her own way. Marie noticed how Frances lingered a little longer in the living room, fingertips brushing the furniture as if reaching for something unseen. Lynn carried herself differently, quieter than usual, and Marie followed her closely, offering gentle words, reassuring touches, and silent space when needed. Brooke took the loss the hardest. Being the oldest, she had more memories of her great-grandmom, and the bond they shared ran deep. So much grief rested on these young shoulders, losing their mom years before and now their great-grandmother too, and Marie felt the weight of it pressing against her heart. She wanted to hold them steady, to let them feel the truth of their grief while giving them whatever comfort she could offer.

Calls and messages from family continued, now tinged with relief that Sophia's suffering was over, but also heavy with their own grief. Marie answered them with the same gentle patience she had shown for days, carrying both her own sorrow and theirs, feeling the threads of love stretch thin across distance and silence.

In the quiet hours, when the girls were asleep and the house seemed to breathe around her, Marie allowed herself to feel it fully, the ache, the exhaustion, the loss. She wept without restraint. She whispered Sophia's name into the emptiness. She remembered every laugh, every small gesture, every moment of care that had defined a lifetime of love.

Even in grief, life demanded something of her. Meals needed to be made, schedules needed to be remembered, small practicalities that seemed trivial against the enormity of loss. Yet in those routines, she discovered tiny moments of grace, the girls' laughter over breakfast, a phone call from a distant relative sharing a memory of Sophia, a quiet smile from Tom in the kitchen that felt tentative but real.

She knew the funeral would come soon, the faces, the words, the rituals, all of them necessary, all of them public. But right now, in the quiet, in the private aftermath, she began the slow work of learning how to live without her mom, of holding both grief and gratitude in the same hand, of remembering that love does not end when life does. It only changes form.

Marie and the girls, along with Tammy, boarded the plane for New York in silence. Each carried her own grief, her own memories, her own quiet anticipation. The hum of the engines filled the small spaces between them, a backdrop to the thoughts and memories that could not be spoken aloud. Marie held the girls' hands firmly and felt the weight of what they were carrying, not just the journey, but the honor of fulfilling Sophia's final wishes.

When they arrived, family was already gathered, flying in from near and far, all coming together to pay respects and support one another. Marie stepped into the quiet reunion with a mixture of sorrow and gratitude, feeling love and loss weave together once more, each presence a reminder that while

Sophia had passed, her life, her guidance, and her care continued to shape those left behind.

Sophia's final arrangements were exactly as she had planned, the mausoleum, the placement beside her husband, the small, deliberate touches that spoke to a lifetime of thoughtfulness. Marie followed each instruction carefully, honoring her mom's wishes, carrying out the final act of love that Sophia had entrusted to her.

The funeral itself was heavy with quiet dignity. Family, friends, and loved ones spoke softly, tears mingling with whispered memories and shared stories. Marie held the girls close, letting them cling to her as they processed the enormity of the day, the absence that had settled into their lives so suddenly and completely. Even in the ceremony, Marie felt the weight of presence and absence intertwine. She watched the careful placement of her mom's casket, the rituals unfold, and she whispered again, softly, to Sophia, "I love you so much, it's okay to go. I will be okay. Nina is waiting for you with all our loved ones."

Afterward, as the family lingered in quiet conversation, as flowers were placed and final words spoken, Marie allowed herself to breathe a little. The task was done. Sophia's wishes were honored. And though grief pressed down, there was also a profound sense of having carried her mom faithfully to the end.

The return flight home was subdued, each of them lost in thought, quietly processing, quietly beginning the work of life after loss. Marie held the girls' hands, watching their faces, memorizing their expressions and gestures, knowing that they too were carrying pieces of Sophia's love forward.

The house greeted them like a patient witness. Marie unlocked the door, stepped inside, and felt the weight of absence settle around her again. Life would continue, the girls would need her, and she would move forward, step by careful step. But in the quiet moments, she allowed herself to sit with the memory of her mom, to hold both grief and love in the same hand, and to begin the delicate work of learning to live in a world forever changed.

She had expected the house to feel empty. She had not expected what waited inside it.

Tom, Marie's husband, had stayed behind, watching the dogs while she and the girls were in New York. And while Marie had been carrying the weight of the funeral and guiding the girls through goodbye, Tom had made a decision of his own.

He bought a motorcycle.

When she found out, it caught her completely off guard. It was not just the motorcycle itself that upset her. It was the fact that he had done it without talking to her first, without asking how she felt, without checking in during a time when everything in her life already felt fragile.

She had just buried her mother. She was helping three grieving girls find their footing again. She was exhausted in ways she had never known before. And suddenly, she was being asked to accept another change she had not been prepared for.

They talked about it one evening after the house had settled. Marie tried to explain how it made her feel, how she wished he had included her, how she needed to feel like they were still making decisions together. Tom listened and told her he had not meant to hurt her. After so much loss and heaviness, he had wanted something that made him feel free, something that reminded him he was still moving forward. He had not thought about how it would feel to her.

She understood his reasoning, even if it still hurt.

The conversation went on until Marie felt herself growing too tired to keep pushing. Her heart was heavy. Her body was worn down. She simply did not have the strength left to fight another battle.

So she let it go.

Not because it didn't matter or because she agreed, but because she was exhausted from everything she had already carried..

71

Chapter 18
When the House Breathes Again

By early afternoon, the house had settled into a fragile calm. Lynn was still on the sofa, Tyson pressed against her side, her tablet resting on the cushion beside her. The pill Marie had left on the table was gone, the empty cup beside it, a quiet sign that she had taken it without a fight.

Marie didn't say anything at first. She simply gave a small nod, the kind Lynn could accept without feeling watched.

"Alright," Marie said gently, her voice steady in the way Lynn responded to. "Time to start your schoolwork."

Lynn's shoulders tightened for a moment, but the medication had taken the sharpest edge off her anxiety. She let out a slow breath, picked up her laptop, and opened her online school portal. Tyson shifted closer, resting his head on her thigh as if anchoring her in place.

Outside, the familiar hiss of the school bus brakes echoed at the end of the street.

Duchess heard it before anyone else.

She had been waiting by Frances's bedroom door all morning, bolted toward the back gate, nails clicking against the floor. She rushed to the fence, tail thumping wildly, her entire body vibrating with anticipation.

Marie smiled despite the long morning. "She's home."

Lynn glanced up for a second, watching Duchess's excitement through the sliding glass door. A tiny smile tugged at the corner of her mouth, small but real.

Frances came through the gate a moment later, backpack bouncing, her face lighting up the instant she saw Duchess. The Dane pressed her massive head into the girl's chest, whining softly, her tail sweeping the ground in wide arcs.

Frances laughed and wrapped her arms around Duchess's neck. "Hi, baby. I missed you too."

The house felt different instantly, brighter, fuller, steadier. Marie felt the shift settle around her like a warm blanket.

Lynn looked back at her screen, but her shoulders had softened. The tension in the room eased, replaced by the familiar rhythm of the afternoon.

Frances was home. Duchess was whole again. And Lynn, medicated and anchored, was trying.

For now, that was enough.

Frances dropped her backpack by the table and headed straight for the kitchen, the way she always did after school. Marie watched her move with that easy confidence she carried, opening the fridge and grabbing a snack. Tyson followed her, tail swaying gently, happy to have the house full again.

"Did you have a good day?" Marie asked.

Frances shrugged as she peeled open a cheese stick. "It was okay. We had a math quiz. I think I did good." She paused, glancing toward the living room. "How's Lynn?"

Marie followed her gaze. "She's doing better now. It was a rough morning."

Frances nodded, the kind of nod that belonged to someone older than her years. She walked over to the sofa and sat beside her sister, careful not to disturb the dog.

"Hey," she said softly.

Lynn didn't look up, but her fingers paused on the keyboard. "Hey."

For a moment, the two girls sat quietly, the kind of quiet that wasn't heavy or awkward, just familiar. Frances leaned back and stretched her legs out, and Tyson curled himself between them, content to be touching both girls at once.

Marie stood in the kitchen, watching them. These were the moments she held onto, the small ones, the ordinary ones, the ones that reminded her why she kept going even on the hardest days.

She began preparing dinner, the sounds of chopping vegetables mixing with the soft hum of the girls' voices Every now and then, Marie heard Lynn quietly reading through her schoolwork while Frances talked beside her, offering small comments and encouragement in her own way. The afternoon light shifted across the floor, warm and golden. The house, once tense and tight, now felt alive again, not perfect, not easy, but alive.

Marie stirred the pot on the stove and let herself breathe. This was their life, messy, unpredictable, exhausting, but full of love and effort.

Above all, full of trying.

Chapter 19
The Call That Feels Like Home

Dinner was easy that night, the kind of evening where no one felt like cooking. Tom ordered takeout, something everyone liked and something simple. Frances grabbed her food and disappeared into her room almost immediately, already on her phone, already deep in conversation with her friends. Fourteen came with moods, opinions, and a flair for drama, and she carried all of it with her down the hallway.

Lynn finished eating quietly and then settled into her room with her tablet. She had been quiet since the day she came to live with Marie and Tom, her world softer and smaller, but steady in its own way. The medication had helped her focus, and she had made it through her schoolwork earlier without a fight. Marie counted that as a win.

The house slowly shifted into its nighttime rhythm. Tom moved around the living room his back stiff but his presence grounding. The dogs found their places, the older one on the sofa, Duchess stretched out on Frances's bed, waiting for her girl to settle in for the night.

Marie finally sat down, letting the quiet settle around her. The day had been long, but the house was calm now, each person tucked into their own corner of the evening.

Her phone buzzed.

It was Aunt Carmella, Zia, as Marie had called her all her life.

Marie's heart lifted instantly. She answered with a smile she hadn't even realized she had been holding back.

"Hi, sweetheart," her aunt said, her voice warm and familiar, the kind of voice that always felt like home.

Thank goodness for FaceTime. At eighty-seven, Zia still lit up the screen with the same spark she had always had. Her husband, almost ninety-four now, was in the other living room watching his war movies, the same ones he had watched for years. They lived with their oldest son now, safe and cared for, surrounded by family.

Marie cherished these calls. Her aunt had been like a second mother her entire life, the last living link to her mom's generation. They talked about everything, the girls, the dogs, the day, but they always drifted back to the past.

To Italy.

To the war.

To the five sisters growing up together in a world that had been anything but easy.

Her aunt told the stories the way she always did, with detail and heart. She remembered how she and Marie's mom and their sisters had survived those years, how they leaned on each other, how they learned to be strong long before they ever knew they would need to be.

She talked about coming to America in 1960, young and hopeful, and how Marie's mom had flown over when her first baby was born and never left. Two sisters reunited, building a life together in a new country.

Marie listened, soaking in every word. She felt her mother close in those stories, close in her aunt's voice, close in the memories that still lived between them.

When the call ended, the house was quiet again. Frances was still talking in her room, Lynn was settled for the night, Tom was getting ready for bed. The dogs were asleep in their usual places.

Marie sat for a moment longer, letting the warmth of her aunt's voice linger.

Another day was done. Another night was settling in. Tomorrow, she would do it all again.

Chapter 20
Where Grief Wakes First

Marie woke before the sun, the house still wrapped in that heavy, early-morning silence. Tom was snoring softly beside her, the dogs asleep in their usual places, and both girls' doors closed. Nothing dramatic, just stillness, the kind that settled deep in her chest.

She lay there for a moment, listening.

Silence had changed for her. It wasn't peaceful anymore. It felt like something waiting.

Marie slipped out of bed and stepped into the kitchen, the cool floor waking her feet. She poured her coffee, the familiar sound grounding her, and opened the sliding glass door to the patio. The morning air met her with its usual quiet welcome. She lit her cigarette, took a slow sip, and let the warmth settle into her hands.

For a few seconds, everything felt almost normal.

Then she heard it.

A distant ambulance siren, faint at first, then growing louder as it moved through the neighborhood. That sound always found her, no matter how many mornings had passed. It slipped under her skin, straight into the place she tried to keep still.

Her fingers tightened around the mug.

And just like that, she was back there.

Back to the day the phone rang and her world split open.

She could still see it clearly. She and her mom sitting on the porch, enjoying what she thought was an ordinary morning. They were talking about nothing important, the weather, the girls, everyday things that felt safe. The sunlight had been soft. The air had been calm. There had been no warning.

The phone rang.

On the other end, her son-in-law's voice was frantic, breaking.

"She stopped breathing," he shouted. "You need to get here quick. The ambulance is on the way."

Marie didn't remember standing up. She didn't remember what she said. What she remembered was the way her body went cold. Not panic, that came later. This was something deeper. A dread that didn't need words.

She didn't remember much of the drive except that she prayed the entire way. Not calm prayers. Not rehearsed ones. She gripped the steering wheel and whispered her daughter's name over and over, asking God to let this be a mistake.

Red lights. Blurred trees. The sun too bright for what was happening.

When she walked into the emergency room, William stood there pale and shaking, trying to explain what made no sense.

"I turned around and she wasn't breathing," he kept saying. "Frances found her."

Marie remembered the waiting more than anything else.

Not minutes.

Not hours.

Just waiting that felt endless and suffocating, like the world had paused to see how much her heart could take before it broke.

Voices spoke around her. Doctors. Nurses. Words about machines and procedures and things she could not hold onto. The details slipped away almost immediately, but the feeling stayed, that helpless, hollow space opening inside her chest.

She remembered asking if she could see her. She remembered thinking, in one desperate, impossible moment, that if she could just touch her daughter's hand, she could fix it. That love might somehow be stronger than whatever was happening behind those doors.

But love didn't stop it.

The siren outside her house grew louder, then slowly faded as it passed down the street. The sound dissolved, but it left its echo behind, just like it always did.

Marie realized she had been holding her breath.

She exhaled slowly and looked back through the sliding glass door. Inside, the house was still sleeping. Tom. The dogs. The girls. Life, fragile but still there.

That was the cruel thing about grief. The world kept going. Mornings kept coming. Coffee still brewed. Birds still sang. Sirens still wailed for someone else.

But for her, they always meant the same thing.

Some mornings grief came like a wave. Other mornings it settled like fog. But it always arrived before the sun fully rose. It always found her in the quiet.

Marie took another sip of coffee and listened carefully.

A soft creak from inside the house. One of the girls shifting in her sleep.

She held still until she heard it again.

Breathing.

Slow. Steady. Alive.

She closed her eyes for just a second, letting that sound anchor her.

Where grief wakes first, love does too.

Every morning, before the rest of the world stirs, Marie rises to meet them both.

Chapter 21
The Worry She Couldn't Silence

The phone buzzed, Marie didn't even have to look to know what it meant. Her oldest granddaughter, twenty-four and independent, driving like the world was a racetrack and she had somewhere urgent to be. That girl had a lead foot and a stubborn streak that reminded Marie of her daughter in ways that were both comforting and terrifying.

She glanced at the screen anyway.

Just a quick check.

Just to make sure she was safe.

But the truth was, every time she checked, it only made her worry more.

Loss had rewired her. It had taught her how fast life could change, how one phone call could split a world in two.

Frances groaned dramatically from the table, dragging Marie back into the kitchen. "Brooke's probably going to Starbucks again," she said, rolling her eyes. "She drives like she's in Fast and Furious."

Marie tried to smile, but her chest tightened. "I just want her to slow down."

"She's fine," Frances said, already scrolling again. "Brooke always thinks she's invincible."

Marie didn't answer.

She loved that girl fiercely, but the fear lived right under her skin. She had lost too much not to worry.

Behind them, Lynn appeared quietly in the doorway, rubbing her sleeve between her fingers, her eyes still soft with sleep. Frances glanced at her and immediately sighed.

"What?" Frances said. "Why are you staring at me like that?"

"I'm not," Lynn whispered.

"Yes, you are."

And just like that, the bickering began, the same dance they did every morning. Two girls who loved each other but could not help but clash. It drove Marie crazy sometimes, but she knew it was normal. Healthy, even. Kids who felt safe enough to argue were kids who felt secure.

Still, she stepped between them with gentle firmness. "Alright. Enough. It's too early for this."

They quieted, mostly because they respected her.

They were good kids. Smart, A B students. Each carrying their own grief in different ways.

Marie looked at them, at the life she was holding together with both hands, and felt that familiar mix of love and fear wash over her.

She wasn't strict. She was scared, scared of losing anything else, of another phone call, of the world taking what little she had left.

But she also knew this: the girls were her purpose now, her reason to get up and keep going. And Brooke, wild, fast-driving Brooke, was part of that too.

Her phone buzzed again on the counter. Another Life360 notification.

Brooke was on the move.

Of course she was.

That girl never drove anywhere under the speed limit, no matter how many times Marie begged her to slow down.

But it wasn't just the driving. It was everything.

Brooke carried her grief like a shadow, quiet, heavy, always there. Losing her mom had carved something deep into her, something Marie recognized because she carried the same wound. Losing her great-grandmother three years later had cracked her even further.

Some days Brooke was fine, laughing, talking, moving through the world like she was determined to outrun her pain. Other days she could not even get out of bed. The anxiety tightened around her chest until she felt like she could not breathe. The irritable bowel syndrome made it worse, stress feeding the pain, the pain feeding the panic, a cycle she could not escape.

Marie saw all of it. Every high. Every low. Every moment Brooke tried to hide.

She checked the tracker again, even though she knew it would not calm her. It never did. If anything, it made her worry more. But she could not stop. Not after everything she had lost.

Behind her, Frances was still talking. Lynn was still hovering. The dogs were pacing. Tom was still sleeping, unaware of the storm moving through Marie's mind. But her eyes stayed on that little dot on her phone.

Brooke, driving too fast, trying to find her way, trying to survive her grief in the only ways she knew how.

Marie whispered, "Slow down, sweetheart. Please."

Not because she didn't trust her, but because she loved her too much to lose her.

Her phone buzzed again, this time with a message.

Brooke:

"I'm going to DoorDash for a bit."

Marie's stomach tightened.

Of course she was.

Brooke never stopped moving on the days she felt well enough. When she had energy, she pushed herself too hard. DoorDash made Marie nervous for a hundred reasons, the strangers, the neighborhoods, the late hours, the constant in and out of the car, and the way Brooke drove that poor thing like it was indestructible.

Marie typed back carefully.

Marie: "Be careful, sweetheart. Please slow down."

She didn't add the rest. The brakes. The tires. The fear that lived under her skin.

Tom shuffled into the kitchen a few minutes later, still half asleep, coffee already on his mind.

"Morning," he mumbled.

"Morning," Marie replied softly.

He poured his coffee and scrolled for a moment before looking up. "You have your doctor's appointment at noon."

Marie froze.

She had forgotten. Again.

"Right," she said quietly.

Diabetes ran deep on her father's side. She had watched what it did to him. Losing his leg. Losing his strength. Losing pieces of himself before he passed. She knew the risks. She knew the warnings.

And still, she didn't take care of herself the way she should have.

It wasn't because she didn't care, there was simply never time for herself.

Because she was always caring for everyone else.

She skipped meals. Grabbed whatever was quick. Ignored numbers. Pushed through dizziness and fatigue.

"You should eat something," Tom said casually.

She nodded, but her thoughts were already drifting, to Brooke on the road, Frances arguing, Lynn hovering nearby, and the appointment she didn't want to face.

Leaving the house still felt wrong.

For years she had stayed close to her mom, always listening, always afraid something would happen if she stepped away. That fear had carved itself into her bones. It didn't fade just because her mother was gone.

In her room, she dressed slowly.

She brushed her hair, washed her face, and looked at herself in the mirror. A woman who had lived through too much and kept going anyway.

She grabbed her purse and keys and walked to the car.

Inside, she sat for a moment before starting the engine.

Then she talked to them.

To Nina.

To her mom.

"I miss you," she whispered. "Please watch over us."

Then, quietly, "And please watch over Zia too."

She wiped her eyes and backed out. Another day, another responsibility.

Another moment carrying grief in the quiet spaces no one could see.

Chapter 22
The World Outside the House

The drive felt longer than it was, every mile stretching out in front of her. Marie kept her hands tight on the wheel, her thoughts drifting between her daughter, her mom, and her aunt, the way they always did when she was alone. By the time she pulled into the parking lot, her chest felt tight and her breath a little shallow, that familiar edge of unease settling in.

She parked farther from the entrance than she needed to and sat for a moment with the engine off, letting the silence settle. The building looked the same as always, beige walls, glass doors, people coming and going like it was nothing. For them, it probably was. For her, leaving the house still felt like stepping into a world she didn't fully trust.

She reached for her purse, took a slow breath, and opened the door.

The air outside felt different here, too clean and too open. She walked toward the entrance with careful steps, her mind already counting the minutes until she could go back home. Inside, the waiting room was cool and quiet, the faint smell of disinfectant mixing with the soft hum of a television mounted on the wall.

Marie checked in at the front desk, her voice steady even though her nerves weren't. The receptionist smiled politely, handed her a clipboard, and told her to have a seat.

She chose a chair near the corner where she could see the door, the hallway, and the people moving around her. Old habits. Years of watching, listening, staying alert. Years of caregiving that had rewired her instincts.

She filled out the forms slowly, her mind drifting again, back to her father and how diabetes had taken so much from him; back to her mom and the years Marie spent caring for her, back to her daughter, whose absence still felt like a wound that never fully closed. And then to her aunt, and the fear of losing her too.

Marie blinked hard and grounded herself.

A nurse called her name.

Marie stood, smoothing her shirt and steadying her breath. She followed the nurse down the hallway, each step feeling heavier than the last. It was another appointment, another reminder that she had to take care of herself even when it felt impossible. Another moment she wished she could just go back home, back to the place where she felt safe.

But she kept walking, because she had to.

The nurse led her into the exam room, took her vitals, and left her sitting on the paper-covered table. A few minutes later, the doctor stepped in with a gentle smile, the kind he used when he knew someone needed reassurance more than anything else.

"Good to see you, Marie," he said as he sat down. "How have you been holding up?"

Marie gave the answer she always did. "I'm fine."

He glanced at her chart, then back at her face, the way doctors do when they know the truth is somewhere in between.

"You've had a lot on your plate," he said softly. "I know you're taking care of everyone at home. But I want to make sure you're taking care of yourself too."

He looked at her glucose numbers not with judgment, but with concern.

"These readings tell me you're running a little high," he said. "Nothing we can't work with, but it does mean we need to pay attention. You matter, Marie. Your health matters."

Marie looked down at her hands, feeling that familiar guilt rise.

"I know it's hard," he continued, calm and steady. "I know you've been through more loss than most people can imagine. But you're still here, and the people you love need you here. Let's try to make small changes, one step at a time. Nothing overwhelming."

He paused, letting the words settle.

"You don't have to be perfect," he said. "You just have to keep trying. And you're not doing this alone."

Marie nodded, her throat tightening. She wasn't used to anyone worrying about her. She wasn't used to being the one who needed care.

The doctor offered a reassuring smile. "We'll take this slowly. You're doing better than you think."

By the time she got back home, relief and exhaustion had settled over her in that familiar mix she always carried after being away longer than she liked. Frances was already at school. Lynn was in her room. The dogs started barking the moment Marie stepped inside, their usual greeting whenever she returned.

She set her purse down and walked straight through the house to the patio, the one place she could breathe for a moment. She sat in her chair, lit a cigarette, and let the smoke curl into the air as she tried to settle her nerves. Being out in the world always left her feeling stretched thin, like she had been holding her breath the entire time.

Her phone rang.

Tammy.

Just seeing the name softened something inside her.

Marie answered, and the moment Tammy spoke, warm, familiar, it felt like the weight on Marie's shoulders eased a little.

"Hey, Marie," Tammy said, her tone bright and steady. "I was thinking about you today."

Marie leaned back in her chair and exhaled slowly. "I'm glad you called."

They didn't talk often, but when they did, it was as if no time had passed at all. The rhythm between them never changed, no matter how long the gap. Tammy had always been the one person who could pull Marie out of her everyday life, even when she had her own hands full with her adult kids.

Marie smiled, the first real one she'd felt all day. "Feels like we just talked yesterday."

Tammy laughed softly. "That's because we never miss a beat."

Marie's mom had loved Tammy, truly loved her. They had connected in a way that felt natural and easy. After her mom passed, knowing Tammy wasn't living close by anymore had added a quiet ache to Marie's days, even though their bond never faded.

Tammy's voice softened. "How are you doing today?"

Marie hesitated, then answered honestly in the way she only could with Tammy. "I'm managing. Had a doctor's appointment. You know how I get."

"Oh, Marie," Tammy said gently, full of understanding. "I wish I was there. I'd take you out for lunch and make you forget everything for a little while."

Marie let out a small laugh, the kind that came from deep inside. "You always knew how to do that."

"That's because you never let yourself breathe," Tammy said. "You carry everyone. Someone needs to carry you once in a while."

Marie closed her eyes and let the words settle. Tammy always had a way of saying exactly what Marie needed to hear, even when she didn't want to admit it.

For a moment, sitting on the patio with the cigarette burning between her fingers and Tammy's voice in her ear, the world felt a little lighter.

When they ended the call, Marie held the phone in her hand for a moment after Tammy's voice faded. Talking to her always loosened something inside her, easing the tightness she carried through the day.

Marie took one last drag from her cigarette, crushed it out in the ashtray, and stood. The patio felt quiet again, the kind of quiet that settles after a good conversation. She slipped her phone into her pocket and stepped back inside.

The rhythm of the house met her immediately.

Chapter 23
The Roads That Made Her

Lynn was in the living room, curled up with her tablet, Tyson trailing behind her like a shadow. Duchess barked once and then settled, recognizing Marie's return. The dishwasher hummed in the background, a steady reminder of the chores waiting for her. A faint smell of laundry detergent drifted from the washer, another task she would get to when she could.

Marie walked over to Lynn, her steps soft, her presence gentle.

"You doing okay?" she asked.

Lynn nodded without looking up, Tyson settling at her feet. "Yeah," she said quietly.

Marie gave a small, warm smile. "Alright. I'm here."

She moved back into the kitchen, letting the familiar comfort of the house wrap around her. This was where she felt safest, where she felt needed, where the world made sense again after being out in it.

The appointment was behind her. The worry about Brooke still lingered, but that was nothing new. Lynn was calm. The dogs were settled. The house was steady.

Marie exhaled slowly and let herself fall back into the rhythm she knew best, caring, watching, moving through the day one small task at a time, holding her family together with quiet, steady hands.

She reached for a dish towel, ready to wipe the counter, when her phone rang.

She didn't need to look. She knew that ringtone.

Zia.

Marie answered, her voice softening instantly. "Hi, Zia."

"Oh, my Marie," her aunt said, her accent warm and familiar, carrying a lifetime of love and history. "I was thinking about you. I wanted to hear your voice."

Marie leaned against the counter and closed her eyes for a moment. "I'm glad you called."

"You sound tired," Zia said gently. "How was your morning?"

"I had a doctor's appointment," Marie said, keeping her tone light. "Just routine."

Zia hummed knowingly. "You take care of yourself, Marie. You hear me? You have to stay strong for those girls."

"I know," Marie whispered.

There was a pause, the kind that only existed between two people who shared a lifetime of memories. Marie could picture Zia in her favorite chair, sunlight on her face, her hands folded in her lap.

Zia's voice softened. "Your mom would be proud of you. She always said you had her strength."

Marie swallowed hard. "I miss her."

"I know, Marie," Zia said quietly. "I miss her too. And I miss your daughter. They are together now, watching over you."

Marie blinked back the sting in her eyes. "I hope so."

Another quiet pause followed.

Zia exhaled, not sadly, but with the weight of honesty. "It's true, Marie. I am getting older. Some days I feel it more than others. Marie's breath caught. "Zia, please…"

"I am here today," Zia said gently. "I am here now. And I love you. That is what matters."

Marie pressed her hand to her chest, grounding herself. "I love you too."

They talked a little longer, about the weather, about a story from Italy Zia had told a hundred times but Marie never tired of hearing. When they finally said goodbye, Marie held the phone for a moment, letting the warmth of her aunt's voice linger.

When she set it down, the house felt fuller, wrapped in memory and love and the fragile comfort of still having someone who called her "my Marie."

She took a slow breath and stepped back into the kitchen, ready to move through the rest of the day.

She believed she understood hardship by then.

She had learned how to manage worry, how to hold grief without letting it spill, how to keep a household steady even when her own heart felt unsettled. She thought she understood what it meant to endure.

But the kind of hardship that reshapes you does not announce itself gently. It does not arrive when you are ready.

It arrives early.

Long before you know who you are.

Chapter 24
Finding a Rhythm

The house had not changed, but everything inside it felt different. Marie moved through familiar rooms with a new awareness, listening to the echoes of absence and the whispers of memory. Each corner held a shadow of Sophia, the gentle hum of her voice, the careful placement of her things, the way she had loved this house so completely.

The girls were still fragile, each moving in her own quiet way. Frances lingered in her room with Duchess, as if her dog could fill what had been lost inside. Lynn returned to her tablet and sketches, finding solace in the lines and colors that had always been her refuge. Brooke, though still heavy with grief, began speaking of Sophia aloud, her voice breaking sometimes, steadying others, as if telling the story could anchor her heart.

Marie watched them closely, always watching, always adjusting, always making sure they felt safe. She moved with gentle patience, listening when they spoke, sitting quietly when they could not, holding them close when the ache became too heavy to bear alone.

Daily life resumed in small, careful steps. Marie found herself returning to the basics, laundry folded and put away, schedules checked twice, ordinary tasks that steadied the girls and kept the days from tipping too far into the quiet. She noticed the quiet beauty in these ordinary acts, how they grounded her, how they served as small threads connecting the girls to the rhythm of living, even as their hearts remained fractured.

Tom's motorcycle still sat between them like an unfinished conversation It was not the motorcycle itself that hurt most, it was the fact that he had not talked to her first. Marie was too exhausted to fight the way she wanted to, so she swallowed the shock and tried to keep her focus where it belonged, on the girls, on the house, on making it through the day on the quiet routines that tethered them to one another.

But she could not ignore the anger and disappointment that lingered, coiling quietly beneath her careful control.

Even so, she found moments of peace. A shared laugh over a memory of Sophia, a phone call from a distant cousin who remembered her mom's humor, a quiet smile from Tom in the kitchen that felt tentative but real, each one a small reminder that life, though forever altered, still held light.

Marie began to carve time for herself as well, moments to sit in the stillness, to write, to remember, to breathe. She discovered that grief could coexist with love, that sorrow could live alongside hope, and that moving forward did not mean leaving Sophia behind. It meant carrying her memory, her lessons, and her love, folded carefully into each day.

At night, when the girls were asleep, Marie would sit on the patio, feeling the quiet settle over the house. She allowed herself to think of Sophia not just in absence, but in presence, in the ways she had shaped their lives, in the way her love continued to ripple through them, and in the legacy of care, strength, and warmth that Marie now carried.

Step by careful step, they began to navigate life again. It was slow, uneven, and heavy at times, but it was theirs. And in those small movements forward, Marie found something profound, a fragile, enduring hope that love, even when touched by loss, could continue to guide them, sustain them, and remind them that life, though different, was still theirs to live.

Across town, William was trying to rebuild a life that no longer made sense. Marie did not see his hardest moments, but she saw enough in his eyes on weekends, in the way he lingered at the door, in the way his voice changed when the girls mentioned their mother. Even as he tried to hold himself together for the girls, he felt the weight of grief pressing down, a constant reminder of what had been taken too soon.

Yet life was insisting on moving forward. William had met someone, a woman named Ann, who brought warmth, understanding, and patience into his carefully guarded world. She was steady where he faltered, caring where he had become exhausted by grief, and she did not rush him or demand that he forget. Slowly, cautiously, William began to let her into the corners of his life that had remained untouched since his wife's passing.

Introducing her to the girls had been delicate work. Ann had already been a presence in their lives before Sophia's condition worsened, someone familiar, someone kind, someone who fit gently into the rhythm of family without forcing herself into the spaces that belonged to those they had lost. William knew he needed to continue honoring that trust, showing the girls that Ann was a friend and support, never a replacement, and letting the relationships grow at their own pace.

Marie watched these interactions quietly, noting how the girls responded, small gestures, shy smiles, tentative questions. She understood the balance William had to strike, honoring the memory of his wife, maintaining the girls' trust and comfort, and continuing to weave Ann gently into their lives.

Life after loss, Marie reflected, was never simple. It was a careful negotiation of love and grief, of boundaries and hope, of remembering those who were gone while making room for those who could still walk beside them. And in the quiet moments, she noticed that even in the fragility of new beginnings, there was a thread of resilience, the promise that life, though forever changed, could still hold connection, care, and even love again.

Over the weeks, the weekend visits became a quiet rhythm of their own. Frances would slowly move out from behind the protective circle of her Great Dane, letting Ann sit beside her on the couch, listening as she read aloud from a favorite book. Lynn, once hesitant, began sharing her sketches with Ann, offering explanations of the lines and colors, and sometimes pausing to smile at Ann's gentle encouragement. Brooke, the most expressive of the three, would recount memories of Sophia, weaving in small observations about Ann, the way she laughed, the way she listened, the way she never tried to replace anyone.

Marie watched it all with careful attention, aware that this delicate balance required patience. She noticed how the girls tested boundaries, how William learned to listen more than he spoke, and how Ann navigated her new role with quiet sensitivity. There were moments of tension, Frances pulling back, Lynn retreating to her sketches, Brooke expressing frustration or sadness, and moments of warmth, laughter, and connection. Marie stayed nearby, guiding, supporting, but mostly letting the family find its own fragile way.

The house felt lighter during the weekends, even though it was not theirs entirely. It was a blend of past and present, Sophia's memory, the girls' grief, William's cautious attempts at rebuilding, and Ann's patient presence, all weaving together in subtle, sometimes messy patterns. Marie realized that love and family were not static, that they were flexible, growing with the needs of those who lived within them.

By the end of each visit, when William and Ann drove back across town, the girls would settle into their routines again, carrying with them the small gifts of connection and reassurance. Frances might curl up with Duchess and whisper about the story Ann had read. Lynn would return to her sketches with a faint smile. Brooke would recount the weekend's moments, sometimes laughing, sometimes teary, but always with the sense that they had survived, together.

Marie moved carefully among them, offering support when needed and space when it was requested. She realized that life after loss was not about rushing to return to normal, but about honoring the rhythms of grief, of memory, and of slow, steady rebuilding. Weekends might bring the presence of William and Ann, but the days in between were where Marie held the threads together, the quiet, constant work of keeping the family steady, resilient, and connected.

In these quiet, ordinary moments, Marie began to feel the faint stirrings of hope, hope that the girls could navigate their grief, that William could rebuild his life gently, and that new love, patient, understanding, and unhurried, could find its place alongside the ones they had lost.

They were not rushing. They were not forgetting. They were learning, slowly, that life could still hold connection and care, even in the shadow of grief.

Chapter 25
The Women Who Made Her

That night, the air outside felt heavier than usual, thick with humidity and the distant promise of rain. Marie sat on the patio, a cigarette burning slowly between her fingers, the ember glowing in the dark like a tiny heartbeat. Her phone rested in her lap for a long time before she finally picked it up and called her aunt.

The call connected after two rings.

"Marie," her aunt said, warm, familiar, steady.

They talked the way they always did, slowly, gently, letting the conversation wander where it needed to go. The girls. The weather. Food. Small things that felt safe before grief found its way into the space between them.

Then, like it sometimes did, the conversation shifted.

"I was thinking about your mom today," her aunt said.

Marie closed her eyes, leaning back in her chair. "Yeah?"

There was a soft exhale on the other end of the phone, the kind that carried years inside it.

"Do you remember when she was on the hospital board in New York?"

Marie let out a small breath. "I remember the parties. I remember her getting dressed up."

Her aunt chuckled softly. "I used to make those dresses, you know."

Marie opened her eyes. "You did?"

"Yes," her aunt said. "I would sew them for her. Beautiful gowns. Silks, satins, sometimes lace if I could find good lace. I wanted her to walk into those rooms and look like she belonged there. Because she did."

Marie swallowed.

"I remember one," her aunt continued, her voice softer now, drifting into memory. "Floral, with spaghetti straps. Simple but elegant. Your mom stood in front of the mirror and said she felt like somebody important."

Marie felt her throat tighten.

Suddenly, she was ten years old again. She could see herself standing in the doorway of her mom's closet, staring at that dress hanging carefully in the garment bag. Waiting until her mom was busy in the kitchen, then slipping inside like she was entering somewhere sacred.

She remembered pulling the dress over her head, the fabric cool and soft against her skin, far too long for her small body. She grabbed one of her mom's high heels, wobbling as she tried to walk across the floor. In her mind, she was not playing dress-up. She was going to the party. Pretending she belonged there. Pretending she was her mom.

Marie let out a shaky breath.

"She was important," she whispered.

"I know," her aunt said. "But sometimes, women like us don't always get told that. So, I made sure she looked like she knew it when she walked into those rooms."

Marie pictured it now, clearer than she had in years. Her mom, younger, alive in a way grief sometimes tried to erase. Strong. Beautiful. Certain in ways Marie had only fully understood after she was gone.

"She used to call me before those parties," her aunt went on. "She would say, 'Is this one good enough?' And I would tell her, 'You were good enough before the dress. The dress just helps other people see it.'"

Marie pressed her lips together, tears sliding quietly into her hairline.

"She was so proud of you," her aunt said gently. "Of the woman you became. Of the mom you are."

The night felt very still around her.

"I wish I could tell her things," Marie whispered. "I wish I could call her and just… talk."

"I know," her aunt said. "I do too."

They sat in that silence together, miles and years apart, but connected by the same woman, the same memories, the same love.

After the call ended, Marie stayed outside a long time. She thought about her mom in those gowns. About being ten years old, wobbling in shoes too big for her feet. About pretending to be strong before she even understood what strength really meant.

She thought about her daughter. About the life she never got to fully step into. About all the versions of her that would never get to exist.

The grief moved through her, familiar now. Not lighter, just known, something she had learned how to carry. And out here, under the heavy night sky, Marie understood something her aunt had been trying to tell her without saying it directly. She came from women who built beauty even when life was hard, women who showed up anyway, women who carried families forward even when their own hearts were heavy.

And now, whether she felt ready or not, she was one of them.

Brooke was building her own life while still carrying everything the family had been through. She had moved into the in-law apartment, the same space her great-grandmother had lived in. The first few nights, she barely slept. The silence felt too full, too familiar, as if she listened too closely, she might still hear oxygen machines, soft voices, whispered goodnights.

Slowly, Brooke began making the space her own. New blankets, new scents, little decorations, music playing sometimes, low and steady, like she was reminding herself she was alive, that life was still moving forward. She was also navigating something new, a relationship, a boyfriend who was kind and patient and trying to understand a family built on deep love and deep loss.

Some nights, Brooke would step outside onto the patio, asking softly, "You mind if I sit?" Marie always shook her head.

They did not always talk. Sometimes Brooke scrolled through her phone. Sometimes she talked about work, her boyfriend, normal things, about life moving forward in ways that sometimes felt almost wrong when grief was still sitting so close.

And Marie let her.

Because Brooke deserved a life that was not built only around loss.

Sometimes, the deeper moments came without warning.

"I still expect to see them sometimes," Brooke said one night.

"Me too," Marie replied.

"I talk to them sometimes. I know that sounds weird."

"It doesn't," Marie said. And she meant it.

Marie began to understand something slowly, quietly. Her aunt was her connection to everything behind her. Brooke, in her own searching, imperfect, beautiful way, was part of everything ahead. And Marie stood between them.

Still grieving. Still learning. Still holding pieces of everyone together.

Some nights, she sat outside until the cigarette burned out. Some nights, she stayed long enough to feel something steady settle inside her.

And under the quiet sky, Marie allowed herself to exist in the space between who she had been, who she had lost, and who she was still becoming.

Chapter 26
Between Then and Now

By morning, the rain had settled into a steady, quiet rhythm against the house, the kind that made everything feel slower, softer, almost suspended in time. Marie woke before the alarm, her eyes opening to the dim gray light filtering through the curtains. For a moment, she didn't move. She just listened, the rain against the roof, the distant hum of traffic somewhere beyond their neighborhood, the quiet breathing of a house still holding sleep.

Then responsibility returned, not loudly, not all at once, but the way it always did, one thought at a time. Dogs to attend to. Making sure Frances was up for school.

She pushed the covers back and sat up slowly, pressing her feet into the carpet, grounding herself in the simple, steady reality of another day she had been given to live. Not the life she once imagined, but the life that was still hers. The house would be waking soon. And Marie would step into it, the same way she always had, present, tired, still healing, still carrying love forward, one ordinary morning at a time.

Days became weeks in a way Marie barely noticed at first. Time didn't pass cleanly. It stretched and folded in strange ways, grief marking some moments sharply while others slipped past almost unnoticed. The rain gave way to clear mornings, then to colder ones, then to days warm enough to open the windows again. Life, steady and persistent, kept moving forward.

The house was learning how to breathe again. Frances laughed more easily on some afternoons, especially when Duchess followed her around like a loyal shadow. Lynn disappeared into her tablet and sketchbooks, building worlds out of color and line, sometimes showing Marie pieces without saying much, just offering them like small windows into her heart. Brooke moved between work, her relationship, and the slow process of building a life that was hers, even while carrying everything that had shaped her.

Grief was still there, but it wasn't the only thing in the room anymore. Marie found herself sitting outside less out of necessity and more out of habit. Some nights she still smoked. Some nights she just sat, breathing, listening to the sounds of a house full of life.

Anthony called often, sometimes just to check in, sometimes to talk about nothing at all. The normalcy of it felt strange at first, then comforting. Her aunt still called too, their conversations stretching long and slow, filled with memories, recipes, family stories, and quiet reassurance that history didn't disappear just because someone was gone.

Weeks layered into months. The sharp edges of loss didn't disappear, but they shifted, becoming something she could carry instead of something that carried her. Marie started planning further ahead again, school events, vet appointments, birthdays coming sooner than she expected. The future no longer felt like something she had to survive minute by minute. It felt uncertain, but possible.

And then, slowly, without fanfare, life began to widen again. Not with announcements or declarations, but with quiet reminders of presence, William calling to check on the girls, asking about school, asking if the dogs were behaving. Sometimes he spoke with Marie, sometimes only with the girls. His voice softer now, as if grief had worn down the sharper edges of him.

Ann had come into his life slowly, carefully, at a time when he wasn't looking for anything except a way to feel less alone. She was patient and kind, understanding in a way that didn't demand explanations, and Marie saw that. For that, she was grateful.

Weekend visits became more natural. Not forced. Not complicated. Just time. The girls would come home talking about dinners across town, movies on the couch, small ordinary moments that now felt important in ways none of them said out loud.

Marie listened. She watched. The protective part of her stayed alert, always making sure the girls felt safe and steady. But she also saw something else, their father was trying. Not perfectly, not without mistakes, but trying in the only way people who have been broken open by loss sometimes can. And the girls were learning something too, that love didn't replace love. It made room for more of it.

Slowly, without anyone naming it, the shape of their family widened. Not the same. Never the same. But still a family. Still connected. Still moving forward, even when it sometimes felt like learning how to live all over again.

Chapter 27
What Marie's Inner Voice Sounds Like

The house was finally quiet. Not the daytime quiet filled with movement and routine. This was the deep, late-night quiet, the kind that settled into the walls and made every thought louder. No doors opening. No voices calling her name. No dogs waiting for her to take them out. Just stillness.

Marie stepped onto the patio and closed the sliding door behind her, letting the night air wrap around her like a thin blanket. She sat in her usual chair, the one with the cushion that had faded from the sun, and lit a cigarette. The ember glowed bright for a moment, then softened as she let it burn between her fingers.

This was the part of the day no one ever saw. The part where she stopped being "strong." The part where she wasn't the caretaker, the problem-solver, the steady one. The part where she was just tired.

Her shoulders dropped the moment she sat down, the weight she carried all day finally slipping into the open. She leaned back and let her head rest against the chair, her eyes drifting toward the dark yard.

If someone could hear inside her head right now, it would sound like this:

Did I do enough today?

Did I miss something?

Are the girls really okay?

What if I mess this up?

What if I'm not enough for them?

Mom, I wish you were here.

Nina, I'm trying. I promise I'm trying.

I'm so tired.

I can't be tired.

They need me.

I'll rest later.

I always rest later.

She took a slow drag, the smoke curling upward into the warm Florida night. The yard was so still it felt like the whole neighborhood had gone to sleep at once, the silence steady and relentless, filling the space she didn't know how to sit in.

Her body ached in places she never talked about, the kind of ache that came from years of lifting, helping, worrying, surviving. Her chest felt tight, not from the cigarette, but from the memories that lived there.

Her mom's voice.

Her daughter's laugh.

The sound of two people she loved more than anything, now gone from the house but never from her mind.

Some nights she swore she could still hear them. A footstep. A sigh. A whisper of movement in the hallway. Grief had a way of echoing.

She closed her eyes and let the memories come. Her mom calling her name from the bedroom. Her daughter's bright smile in the kitchen. The way the house used to feel full, chaotic, loud, alive.

Now the quiet felt too big.

Marie rubbed her thumb over the edge of the chair arm, grounding herself. She didn't cry. She rarely did. The tears stayed tucked somewhere deep, behind the part of her that had learned to keep moving no matter what.

But the ache, that stayed.

She thought about the girls, their routines, their struggles, their needs. She thought about Lynn's quiet mornings and Frances's soft heart. She thought about the dogs, the house, the bills, the endless list of things she had to hold together.

She thought about her brother in New York, alone and calling every day because she was the only person he had left.

Everyone needed something from her, and she gave it.

Every day. Without fail.

But out here, in the dark, she allowed herself to admit the truth.

She was exhausted, not the kind of tired sleep could fix, but the kind that lived deep in her bones.

She took another drag, exhaled slowly, and whispered into the night, "I'm doing my best."

No one heard her.

But she needed to say it anyway.

The cigarette burned down to the filter. She crushed it out and stared at the yard for a long moment, letting the quiet settle again.

As she sat there, staring into the dark yard, her thoughts drifted somewhere she didn't let them go very often. She thought about the girls' futures, the parts of life that were still unwritten. Graduations. Weddings. First homes. Babies of their own. The kinds of milestones that mark a life in ways both beautiful and irreversible.

Her heart tightened when she thought about who wouldn't be there.

Their mother should have been standing in the front row at those graduations. She should have been the one helping zip wedding dresses and crying through vows. Their great-grandmother should have been there too, offering quiet advice and steady reassurance the way only she could. The thought of those empty spaces still broke something inside her.

But then another thought rose gently behind it.

She would be there.

She would sit in those folding chairs and clap too loudly. She would hold tissues in her purse and pretend she wasn't crying. She would stand beside them in hospital rooms, waiting to meet their babies, telling them they were stronger than they realized. She would walk with them through every milestone she was given the gift to witness.

She couldn't erase the absence of the women who came before her, but she could make sure the girls never walked into those moments alone.

That realization didn't take away the ache. It didn't make the losses smaller. But it warmed something in her chest all the same. It reminded her that love did not disappear when someone was gone. It changed shape. It shifted hands. It kept moving forward through whoever was still standing.

And whether she felt ready or not, she was one of the ones still standing.

She took a slow breath and let that settle into her bones.

Tomorrow would come. The girls would wake up. Life would continue in all its small, relentless ways. But one day, when those bigger moments arrived, she would be there.

Not instead of the women they had lost.

But because of them.

Tomorrow she would get up and do it all over.

Because that's what she did.

That's who she was.

But for now, for this one small sliver of night, she let herself be human.

Chapter 28
Showing Up

The next morning came the way mornings always did, without asking anyone if they were ready. A pale strip of light slipped through the curtains, stretching slowly across the bedroom wall. Marie opened her eyes before the alarm, the way she often did now, her body trained to wake before the day could get ahead of her. For a moment, she lay still, listening to the house, the soft hum of the refrigerator, the faint shift of Tyson adjusting on his bed, and the quiet breathing of a home still suspended between night and responsibility. Last night lingered in her chest, not sharp or overwhelming, just present, a quiet understanding she had carried with her into morning.

She rose slowly and pressed her feet into the carpet, grounding herself in something solid and ordinary. There were dogs to let out and a school morning waiting to unfold. Life did not pause because she had reached some realization on the patio. It simply folded that realization into the next day and kept moving.

In the kitchen, she started the coffee and opened the sliding glass door for Tyson. The morning air was cooler than it had been lately, a thin breeze carrying the faint scent of damp earth from the night before. She watched him wander into the yard, his familiar shape moving through the early light, and felt a steadiness settle into her shoulders.

Frances came in first, not rushing, not being dramatic, but quiet in a way that felt heavier than usual. Her hair was tangled from sleep, one sleeve of her sweatshirt slipping down over her hand as she walked to the table and sat without speaking, staring at nothing in particular. Marie noticed immediately. Of course she did. She set a mug down gently and studied her granddaughter's face without making it obvious.

"Morning," she said softly.

Frances nodded, eyes still lowered. "Morning."

There was something underneath the word. Not anger. Not defiance. Something smaller and more fragile. Marie felt her old instinct rise immediately, fix it, ask questions, fill the silence, make it better. Instead, she poured herself a cup of coffee, sat down across from her, and waited.

The clock ticked faintly on the wall. Outside, the dog scratched at the door, waiting to be let in. A car passed down the street.

Finally, Frances spoke.

"I don't want to go today."

Marie kept her voice steady. "Something happen?"

Frances hesitated, then shrugged in that way teenagers do when the weight feels too big to explain all at once. "It's just…" she began, then stopped, tracing a small circle on the table with her fingertip, as if the answer might appear there. Marie didn't rush her.

"It's been weird lately," Frances said finally. "At school. With people talking about stuff. Families. Moms helping with things." She lifted one shoulder slightly. "I don't really talk about mine."

Marie felt the familiar tightening in her chest, but kept her face calm. "I know," she said gently.

Frances glanced up. "You do?"

"Yes. You've always carried that part pretty quietly."

Relief softened her face. "I don't want people feeling sorry for me," she admitted. "And I don't want to make it a whole thing. So, I just don't say much."

Marie took a slow sip of coffee, giving her space.

"And Ann…" Frances continued. "She's been nice. Like, really nice. Not fake. Not trying too hard." She hesitated. "I like being there sometimes. It feels normal. But then I feel bad for liking it."

"Bad how?" Marie asked.

"Like I'm doing something wrong. Like I'm forgetting Mom."

Marie leaned forward slightly. "Liking someone new doesn't erase your mom," she said firmly. "Nothing ever could."

Frances studied her face and found no doubt there.

"You're allowed to have good things," Marie added. "You're allowed to feel comfortable. You're allowed to care about people who care about you."

"It still feels strange," Frances whispered.

"It probably will for a while," Marie replied. "That doesn't mean it's bad."

She stood to let the dog in, then returned to her seat.

"You don't have to figure all of this out right now," she continued. "You're still growing. Still becoming who you're going to be."

Frances was quiet for a moment. "I'm glad I can talk to you about this," she said. "I was afraid you wouldn't understand."

Warmth bloomed in Marie's chest. "I'm glad you trusted me enough to come to me," she replied.

Lately, Frances had been asking more often to go to her dad's house. She always said it was to spend more time with him, and Marie knew that was partly true. But she also knew Frances liked being around Ann. At first, Marie hadn't been comfortable with it, not because of Ann, but because of Frances's need to control situations and decide how things should go.

That worried her.

She reached across the table and rested her hand over Frances's. "Sweetheart," she said quietly, "sometimes life doesn't work the way you plan."

Frances listened.

"I'm the adult," Marie continued gently. "You're still learning. You don't have to carry everything."

Frances frowned. "But what if I know what I want? What if I'm right?"

Marie smiled softly. "There it is. That stubborn streak. Straight from your mama."

"I'm not stubborn."

"You just argued about being stubborn."

"That's different."

Marie laughed softly. "No, sweetheart. That's exactly what it is."

Frances crossed her arms. "I just don't like people deciding things for me."

"I know," Marie said. "And one day, you'll decide everything."

"Really?"

"Really."

Frances tilted her head. "I still think you're wrong sometimes."

Marie smiled. "I'm sure you do."

"But… I know you're trying to help."

"That's all I ask."

Frances stood and slipped on her backpack. "I'm still wearing the hoodie I want."

"I figured."

"Love you."

"Love you more."

After she left, Marie sat quietly with her coffee, smiling to herself. That tone, that stubborn lift of the chin, that courtroom-style arguing, it wasn't just personality.

It was Nina.

Chapter 29
The Empty Chair

The invitation had been sitting on the counter for three days before Marie finally picked it up and read it for the third time. Middle School A–B Honor Awards Night. Auditorium. Parents and guardians welcome. She traced her thumb along the edge of the paper, feeling that familiar tightening in her chest. This was one of many awards the girls had earned over the years, and yet this one felt different, another milestone, another moment Nina should have been here for, and the first one her mom would not be there to see.

Frances had pretended not to care. "It's dumb," she had said, tossing her backpack onto the couch. "It's just some stupid assembly." But Marie had seen the truth in the small things, the way Frances asked what time it started, the way she laid out three different outfits and claimed she hated every one of them, the way she checked the clock more than once without admitting why.

So now, standing in the kitchen with the invitation in her hand, Marie already knew this night would matter more than Frances was willing to admit.

"Grandma?" Frances called from her room. "What time are we leaving?"

"In about forty-five minutes," Marie replied.

"Okay," Frances said, too quickly, too tight.

Marie folded the invitation and slipped it into her pocket, then walked toward Frances's room. She knocked lightly. "Can I come in?"

"Yeah."

The room looked like a small tornado had passed through it. Clothes were spread across the bed, shoes lined up against the wall, her backpack half-open on the floor. Frances stood in front of the mirror, tugging at the sleeves of her floral dress, her brow furrowed.

"I don't know if I look stupid," she said.

"You don't," Marie replied gently.

"You're just saying that."

"I'm really not. You look nice. You look like you."

Frances twisted slightly, studying herself. "Ann said this dress looks good on me."

Marie felt something flicker in her chest, quick and unexpected, but she kept her voice steady. "She's right."

"You're not mad, right?" Frances asked quietly.

"About what?"

"About… me liking her."

Marie crossed the room and straightened the shoulders of her dress. "No, sweetheart. I'm not mad. I'm glad you have people who care about you."

Frances nodded, still uncertain. "Okay," she said after a moment. "Let's go before I change my mind."

William and Ann were already waiting in the parking lot when Marie and Tom pulled in. The girls piled out of the car together, backpacks slung over their shoulders, voices overlapping as they pointed toward the auditorium. Marie stayed seated for a moment, watching them, feeling a quiet swell of pride rise in her chest. They had been through more than most kids their age, and still they showed up, still they worked hard, still they kept going. That mattered.

Inside, the school buzzed with families. Parents and grandparents filled the hallways, voices echoing off the walls, cameras ready. The smell of floor cleaner and popcorn drifted through the air, familiar and oddly comforting.

They found their way into the auditorium and shuffled into a row near the front. Marie sat between Tom and Lynn, who bounced her knee restlessly.

"Stop," Brooke whispered, smiling. "You're gonna shake the whole row."

Marie settled into her seat and adjusted her purse on her lap. She glanced down the row automatically, counting heads the way she always did.

Tom.

Lynn.

Brooke.

William.

Ann.

And then she saw the empty seat.

It sat between William and Tom, folded up neatly, untouched, as if it had been waiting for someone who had simply stepped away. Her breath caught before she could stop it. That chair should have been filled. Her mom would have been there, leaning forward too much, whispering questions, clapping too loudly. Nina would have been beside her, phone out, already crying before Frances even reached the stage.

Marie could see it so clearly it almost hurt.

She folded her hands together and stared at the stage, forcing herself to breathe normally. No one else seemed to notice the empty seat, but she felt the weight of it settle into her chest. She reached down and rested her hand lightly on Tom's lap, grounding herself.

You're here, she told herself. You're here for her.

And she was. She would always be. Still, for a moment, she let herself miss them.

Frances was backstage, waiting for her name to be called. The lights dimmed, and the ceremony began. Names were read. Students walked across the stage. Applause rose and fell in steady waves.

Marie listened, her hands folded in her lap, her heart quietly counting down.

Then she heard it.

"Frances Miller."

Her breath caught as Frances walked out from behind the stage, trying to look calm and failing just a little. Her cheeks were pink, her steps quick.

Their whole row erupted with pride. Marie clapped until her palms stung, her eyes blurring as she watched Frances accept her certificate and glance toward the crowd. For half a second, her eyes found Marie's, and she smiled.

Afterward, families spilled into the hallway, laughter and voices filling every corner. Phones were handed around. Arms wrapped tight. Pictures were taken and retaken.

Marie stood beside Frances, arm around her shoulders. "You did amazing," she said softly.

Frances shrugged, but her grin gave her away. "It wasn't hard."

"Sure, it wasn't," Marie replied, smiling.

William took pictures. Ann fixed Frances's hair before another photo. Brooke and Lynn leaned in close, squeezing into the frame. For a moment, everyone was there, laughing, proud, together. Marie held it in her heart like something fragile and precious.

As they gathered their things and walked toward the exit, Marie noticed how naturally Frances fell into step beside William, how Ann leaned in to whisper something that made her laugh, how the three of them moved together without thinking about it. It was easy. Comfortable.

And for a moment, Marie felt both grateful and unsettled. The girls were finding stability again, and their lives were beginning to stretch beyond her in ways she could not control.

She watched them walk ahead, framed by the glow of the hallway lights, and understood that another chapter was quietly opening, one that would ask her to trust, one that would ask her to let go, just a little.

Chapter 30
Making Room

Marie had never worried about being replaced. She knew her place in the girls' lives. She had earned it through sleepless nights, rushed school mornings, doctor appointments, grief, patience, and a kind of love that never clocked out. She was the one who signed permission slips, stayed up when nightmares came, and held everything together when the world fell apart. She was their home, their constant, their safe place. That wasn't changing.

Still, over time, she began to notice small shifts.

Frances would mention something Ann had said in passing. Brooke would talk about conversations she had with her dad and Ann. William's texts slowly changed from "What do you think?" to "Ann thinks this might help." Nothing about it was disrespectful or wrong. It wasn't careless or thoughtless. It was simply new, unfamiliar in a way that made Marie pause and notice.

She became aware of it one evening while folding laundry on the couch. Lynn was sitting at the table, carefully planting seeds she planned to place later in her greenhouse, her tongue slightly poked out in concentration.

"Grandma," Lynn said suddenly, without looking up, "Ann says I'm really good at growing plants."

Marie smiled. "You are."

"She thinks I should start a garden," Lynn added, gently pressing soil into a small container.

Marie paused, a towel still in her hands. "That sounds like a good idea," she said.

"She said she could come over sometime and help me."

Something soft and complicated moved through Marie's chest. It wasn't jealousy. It wasn't fear. It was simply the quiet awareness that things were shifting in ways she hadn't expected.

"That's sweet of her," she replied honestly.

And it was.

Ann wasn't crossing boundaries or overstepping. She wasn't trying to take over or prove anything. She wasn't trying to be someone she wasn't. She was simply showing up, offering kindness, paying attention, and caring in her own gentle way.

Later that night, after the girls had settled into their rooms and the house had grown still, William called.

They talked about ordinary things at first, work, traffic, a bill that needed paying, Frances's latest opinion about school lunches, the way Lynn had become obsessed with watering schedules.

Then he hesitated slightly before saying, "Hey… Ann was wondering if maybe Lynn would want to come over sometime and see her garden. Just get out of the house for a bit."

Marie leaned back in her chair, listening to the hum of the ceiling fan.

"I've been thinking about that too," she said.

"Yeah?" William sounded relieved. "She's been encouraging her a lot lately."

"I've noticed," Marie replied gently.

There was a brief pause, not awkward or uncomfortable, just thoughtful.

"I really appreciate everything you do," William said quietly. "I know none of this works without you."

Marie closed her eyes for a moment, letting the words sink in.

"I know," she said softly. "And I'm glad Ann cares about them."

After the call ended, Marie stepped onto the patio. The night was warm and still, the yard quiet, the air heavy with the sounds of distant insects and soft wind through the trees. She sat in her chair and let herself breathe, really breathe, the way she rarely did during the day.

Ann wasn't taking Nina's place. She wasn't stepping into Marie's role. She wasn't changing the foundation of their family.

She was becoming part of the girls' emotional world, offering them another layer of support, another safe place to land.

And that was a good thing, even if it felt strange sometimes, even if it meant Marie wasn't the only one holding every piece anymore.

She lit a cigarette and watched the dark yard, thinking about Lynn's careful hands in the soil, Frances's stubborn debates, Brooke's quiet strength, and William's steady effort to rebuild something good for their girls.

Maybe making room didn't mean losing anything. Maybe it meant letting something grow.

She took a slow breath and felt it settle inside her.

Letting someone else love them too, without letting go.

Chapter 31
The Voices That Hold Her

The phone rang every morning around the same time. Sometimes it was before Marie finished her first cup of coffee and cigarette. Other times it came while she was doing laundry or sweeping the floors. But it always came.

Her brother.

And later in the day, her aunt.

Without fail.

Marie had come to depend on those calls more than she liked to admit. They had become part of the rhythm of her life, stitched into her days as naturally as meals and schedules and bedtime routines.

That morning, the phone rang while she was standing at the kitchen counter, scrolling through a list of appointments she kept in her daily calendar. She smiled before she even looked.

"Hey," she said, answering.

"Hey, sis," Anthony replied. "You up already?"

"Been up," Marie said. "You know me."

He laughed softly. "Yeah. I do."

They talked about small things at first, the weather in New York, his dog. A friend who talked too much. A spare room he kept putting off cleaning. Ordinary things that only sounded simple on the surface.

Marie could always hear what he didn't say, the loneliness, the quiet apartment, the way life had narrowed for him after losing their parents and his partner.

"How are the girls?" he asked.

"They're good," Marie replied. "Frances is still our drama queen. Lynn's got her plants everywhere. Brooke's working too much, like always."

He hummed thoughtfully. "You're doing a good job with them. You know that, right?"

Marie paused. "I'm trying."

"You always do," he said.

There was pride in his voice, and gratitude, and something close to dependence. She knew she was his anchor now, the one person who still understood where he came from, the one who remembered their childhood, the one who carried the same memories.

After they hung up, Marie stood for a moment with the phone in her hand before setting it down. She took a breath, then went back to her daily calendar.

Later that afternoon, while sunlight slanted through the sliding glass door and the house settled into its quiet hours, her phone rang again. This time, she knew before looking.

"Zia," she said softly.

"My Marie," her aunt replied, warmth filling every syllable. "I was waiting to hear your voice."

Marie smiled and leaned back against the couch. "I was wondering when you'd call."

"You sound tired today," her aunt said gently.

Marie exhaled. "I am. A little."

Her aunt didn't rush to fill the silence. She never did. She understood that sometimes listening was more important than speaking.

"How are the girls?" her aunt asked.

"Growing," Marie replied. "Always growing."

"And you?" her aunt pressed quietly.

Marie hesitated. Then, because it was her aunt, she answered honestly. "Some days I feel strong. Some days I feel like I'm just holding on."

"That is strength," her aunt said. "Holding on is strength."

They talked about family, about memories, about recipes Marie still tried to get right and never quite did, about Italy, about their mother and sisters, about stories that had been told so many times they felt like heirlooms.

"You remind me so much of your mother," her aunt said suddenly.

Marie's chest tightened. "How?"

"The way you carry everyone," her aunt replied. "How you are so head strong. The way you think last of yourself."

Marie laughed softly. "That doesn't sound like a compliment."

"It is," her aunt said. "And it is also a warning."

Marie grew quiet.

"You don't have to be strong every minute," her aunt continued. "Even strong women rest."

"I know," Marie whispered.

"Do you?" her aunt asked gently.

Marie didn't answer right away.

After they hung up, she sat for a long time in the quiet.

She thought about how both of them depended on her in different ways. Her brother needed her steadiness. Her aunt needed her connection. The girls needed her everything. And she gave it, every day, without hesitation.

But sometimes, in those calls, in those familiar voices, she realized something important.

They held her too.

In the sound of Anthony's laughter.

In her aunt's steady wisdom.

In the way they checked on her without making it obvious.

In the way they reminded her she was not alone in this.

That night, sitting on the patio with the house finally quiet, Marie held her phone in her lap and thought about the invisible web that still connected them all, across states, across oceans, across loss, across time. The family didn't disappear; it just rearranged itself. And somehow, she was still standing in the center of it, holding those threads with both hands, not out of obligation, but out of love.

Every day when her aunt called, Marie found herself thinking how grateful she was for one more day with her. Aside from her mother, her aunt had been everything to her. The thought of losing her someday would rise suddenly in her chest, heavy and frightening.

How will I live without her too? What happens then?

The thought crushed her if she let it linger too long.

And then there was her brother in New York. She often wondered how he did it. For so many years, he and his partner Mary had lived together, held each other up, depended on one another. And now, just like that, he was alone.

Marie closed her eyes and took a slow breath.

She didn't have answers for any of it. She only knew that for now, they still had each other.

And she would keep answering the phone.

Every time.

Chapter 32
When the Weight Finally Spills

It happened on an afternoon that should have felt ordinary. There was no emergency, no ringing phone, no crisis waiting at the door. The girls were out, one at school, one at work, one still sleeping. The dogs were asleep, their steady breathing filling the quiet corners of the house. The dishwasher hummed softly in the background. Sunlight filtered through the kitchen window, catching dust in the air and turning it into something almost beautiful.

Everything was handled. Dinner was planned. Laundry was folded. Appointments were written neatly in her calendar. There was nothing pressing, nothing urgent demanding her attention. And that was the problem.

Marie stood at the sink rinsing a coffee cup, watching water run over the porcelain, when she realized she didn't know what to do with herself in the absence of need. Her body was so used to moving toward the next task, the next responsibility, the next person who required something from her, that stillness felt unnatural. She turned off the faucet and set the cup down carefully, her hands remaining on the edge of the counter, fingers curling slightly against the cool surface.

She felt it then, not panic or illness, but a tightness deep in her chest, the kind that builds slowly over years rather than moments.

Her phone buzzed against the counter. A message from Anthony appeared on the screen.

Just checking in. Love you.

She stared at the words longer than necessary. They were gentle and ordinary, but something inside her shifted. She had been holding everyone for so long, the girls, her brother, her aunt, even Tom in quiet ways, that she had forgotten what it felt like to not be the steady one.

She reached for a dish towel and began wiping the counter, though it was already clean. The motion was automatic, almost desperate, as if movement alone might keep whatever was rising inside her from breaking loose. It didn't work.

Her mind began pulling threads she had carefully kept tucked away, the hospital room where Nina lay still and surrounded by machines, the sound of her mother's oxygen at night, the weight of paperwork and decisions, the awards ceremonies where she clapped loudly enough for two missing people, the way the girls' faces searched the crowd for someone who would never be sitting there again.

She swallowed hard and whispered, "I'm fine," to the empty kitchen, the same words she had said to doctors, to family, and herself for years. But she wasn't. She was exhausted in a way sleep could not fix, exhausted from carrying grief so carefully that it never spilled onto the girls, exhausted from being the strong one, exhausted from being needed without pause.

Her breath began to shake. She tried to steady it, the way she had always steadied everything else, but this time her body refused. She slid down slowly against the cabinet until she was sitting on the kitchen floor, her back pressed to the wood, her knees bent in front of her. She hadn't meant to sit. She certainly hadn't meant to cry.

The first tear surprised her. Then another followed, and suddenly years of contained sorrow, responsibility, and unspoken fear broke loose all at once. She covered her face with both hands, not because anyone was there to see her, but because the vulnerability felt almost foreign. She whispered into her palms that she was tired, not tired of loving them, never that, but tired of carrying everything alone.

Her thoughts came in waves, her mother's voice, Nina's laughter, her brother trying to sound stronger than he felt, her aunt's tone softening whenever she asked how Marie was really doing. She thought of the girls, their milestones, their quiet strength, their hidden ache, and she found herself whispering that she had needed them longer, though she didn't know which of them she meant.

For a long time, she let herself cry without stopping it or trying to make it smaller. The house remained quiet around her, holding the sound without judgment. No one needed her in that moment. No one was calling her name. There was no immediate problem to solve. There was only her.

Eventually the storm inside her began to ease. Her breathing slowed. The sharpness dulled. What remained was a heavy but honest stillness. She wiped her face with the sleeve of her shirt and stayed seated on the floor a while longer, letting the quiet settle again. The house had not fallen apart. Nothing had broken. The world had not shifted just because she had allowed herself to unravel for a few minutes.

When she finally stood, her legs felt stiff and her eyes swollen, but something inside her felt different, not fixed or healed, but lighter. She hadn't failed or collapsed. She had simply stopped pretending she could carry everything without ever setting it down. And for the first time in a very long while, she wondered what it might look like to let someone hold her, even for a little while.

She washed her face at the sink, ran cold water over her wrists, and took a slow breath. When she looked in the mirror, her eyes were red and her face tired, but familiar. Still Marie. Still standing.

By the time she heard the garage door open and the dogs lift their heads, she had already smoothed her voice, wiped the counter one last time, and slipped back into herself. No one would know she had sat on the kitchen floor and cried. No one needed to.

She had done what she always did. She gathered herself and kept going.

Chapter 33
The One Who Stayed Close

Tyson had slept beside her bed again, his body curled in the same spot he claimed every night. He didn't stir when she shifted or when the alarm buzzed softly. He waited, the way he always did, until she swung her legs over the side of the mattress. Only then did he rise, slowly and stiffly, but with purpose.

He pressed his shoulder gently against her knee as she stood, as if making sure she was steady before she took her first step. Tyson had always been loyal, but this morning there was something different in the way he stayed close. Closer than usual, close enough that she could feel the warmth of him against her leg with every move she made.

She walked toward the kitchen, and he didn't trot ahead the way he sometimes did. He stayed right beside her.

The house was quiet, every sound carrying through the stillness. Duchess was still asleep in Frances's room, curled against her the way she always did. No footsteps. No voices. Just the soft hum of the refrigerator and Tyson's nails clicking gently on the tile as he followed her.

Marie filled her coffee cup, the kitchen dim in the early hour. No sunlight reached this part of the house yet. But she didn't need it. She knew where she was headed. She needed the patio. The air. The quiet. The small ritual that steadied her before the day began.

She slid open the glass door. Tyson followed, close enough that she could feel his breath against the back of her calf.

Outside, the morning air wrapped around her, cool and familiar. She settled into her usual chair, coffee in one hand, cigarette in the other. Tyson lowered himself at her feet, not stretched out the way he sometimes did, but tucked close, his head resting against her slipper.

He watched her. Not demanding anything. Not restless. Just present. Marie took a slow sip of her coffee. Her chest still felt tender from the day before, from the quiet unraveling she had folded back into herself before anyone came home. She hadn't spoken a word of it. She didn't plan to. She never did.

But Tyson knew. He always did.

She reached down and brushed her fingers over his muzzle. He closed his eyes and leaned into her touch with a soft, contented sigh.

"I'm okay," she whispered.

He didn't move. He didn't pull away. He didn't believe her.

And somehow, in that quiet, wordless understanding, she felt less alone than she had in days.

Marie let her hand rest on Tyson's head a moment longer, her fingers brushing his soft fur. The steadiness of him, the way he stayed pressed close without asking for anything, stirred a thought she had been avoiding for months.

She remembered the way he had stayed beside her mother in those final days. How he had sensed the shift before any of them had. How he had refused to leave her side, even when his hips ached and the floor was cold. How he had laid his head gently against her mother's arm and stayed there for hours, breathing with her, watching her, guarding her in that quiet, loyal way only he could.

Tyson had known then, before any of them were ready to admit it.

And some part of her feared he knew something now too.

The thought tightened her chest, sharp and unwelcome. She blinked hard, looking out toward the yard as if the stillness there could steady her.

"It's okay," she whispered again, though she wasn't sure who she was trying to convince, Tyson, herself, or the memory she had just stirred awake.

Tyson shifted only enough to press closer, his weight warm against her feet, his presence grounding her in a way nothing else could.

Marie took another slow sip of coffee, letting the morning air cool her skin. She didn't push the thought away this time. She let it sit beside her, quiet and heavy, just like the dog who had carried more truth than she ever gave him credit for.

Chapter 34
The Message

It happened on an ordinary afternoon, and that was the strange part. Marie wasn't looking for anything. She hadn't been searching for signs or answers or comfort. She was sitting on the couch with her phone in her hand, half watching a show she had already seen, half scrolling through TikTok the way she sometimes did when her mind felt too full to settle on one thing.

It was just noise and distraction, something to keep the thoughts quiet for a while.

Tyson lay stretched out on the rug nearby, his breathing slow and steady. Duchess was asleep in Frances's room. The house was calm, the kind of calm that felt rare lately, not heavy or tense, just still.

Marie shifted her weight and pulled a blanket over her legs. She wasn't sad or overwhelmed. She wasn't anything, really, just tired in that deep, familiar way that lived under her skin.

She scrolled through another video, another voice, another distraction.

Then a live video appeared on her screen.

A woman sat in front of a simple background, her voice calm, her eyes closed for a moment before opening again. Nothing flashy or dramatic, just a quiet presence.

"Spirit-led," the caption read.

Marie almost scrolled past it. She didn't usually stop for things like that. She didn't usually let herself believe in anything she couldn't touch. But something, she couldn't explain what, made her pause.

She listened.

The woman spoke slowly, carefully, as if choosing each word with intention.

"I have a daughter here with me," she said.

Marie's thumb froze. Her chest tightened, but she didn't react. Lots of people had daughters. It didn't mean anything. She kept watching, telling herself it was coincidence, nothing more.

"She's showing me how her mom talks to her in the car," the woman continued. "Like she's sitting right there in the passenger seat, having full conversations."

Marie's breath caught. Her heart beat faster, not wildly, just enough for her to feel it in her throat. She told herself she was being silly, that grief made you hear what you wanted to hear, that she was reading into it.

Then the woman tilted her head slightly, as if listening to someone just out of frame.

"She's a mother too," she said. "And she's showing me the number three."

Marie felt her phone grow heavy in her hand. Three girls. Her girls. Her fingers began to tremble, but she still didn't type anything.

"She's showing me her oldest," the woman went on. "Very long hair. And her middle one… she's more tomboyish. Strong. Not afraid to be herself."

Marie couldn't breathe. Tears filled her eyes so quickly she didn't even feel them coming. That was Brooke. That was Lynn. That was Frances. That was her life.

Her hands shook as she finally typed into the chat: That's my daughter.

The words blurred as she sent them.

The woman looked down at the screen, nodded slowly, and her voice softened. "She wants you to know she hears you," she said. "When you talk to her in the car. When you ask her things. When you tell her about the girls."

Marie covered her mouth with her hand. She was crying now, fully and silently, the kind of crying that came from somewhere deep and long held, the kind she never let herself feel in front of anyone.

Tyson lifted his head, watching her with quiet concern, but he didn't move. He simply stayed close, steady and present.

"And she says you worry," the woman continued. "You wonder if you're doing everything right. If you're enough for them."

Marie closed her eyes. She didn't need to type anything; the truth of it lived in her chest every day.

"She says yes," the woman whispered. "And thank you. She's proud of you. She's with you and the girls. Always. And she loves you more than you know."

Marie slid down against the back of the couch; her phone pressed to her chest as if holding it closer might hold the moment in place. Her tears came harder now, not from pain or fear, but from the sudden, overwhelming release of being seen, of being answered, of being held by something she hadn't expected.

Tyson rose slowly and came to her side, resting his head on her knee. She placed a trembling hand on his fur, grounding herself in the warmth of him.

The video continued, the woman moving on to someone else, another message, another story, but Marie didn't hear any of it. Her world had narrowed to a single point, the echo of her daughter's love, the one she had carried in her heart for years, suddenly spoken aloud by a stranger.

She stayed like that for a long time, letting the moment wash over her, letting the tears fall freely for once. The world around her faded into the background until there was nothing left but her heart, her daughter, and the quiet, overwhelming feeling that maybe, just maybe, she wasn't as alone as she had believed.

Chapter 35
After the Message

Marie stayed on the couch long after the live ended, her phone still pressed to her chest, her breath coming in slow, uneven waves. She wasn't crying anymore, but the tears had left her drained in a way that felt strangely peaceful, as if something inside her had finally unclenched.

Tyson hadn't moved from her side. His head rested on her knee, warm and heavy, as if he understood she needed the weight of him there. She stroked the top of his head absentmindedly, her fingers moving through the familiar fur.

The house was quiet, the kind of quiet that felt full instead of empty. She leaned her head back against the couch and closed her eyes. She didn't know how long she sat like that, minutes, maybe longer. Time felt different now, stretched thin around her like a blanket she didn't want to disturb.

Eventually she took a deep breath and wiped her face with both hands. Tyson lifted his head, watching her closely.

"I'm okay," she whispered, her voice still thick.

Marie pushed herself up slowly, her body heavy but her mind strangely clear. She walked to the kitchen, Tyson glued to her side, and poured herself a glass of water. Her hands were steadier now. She took a sip, then another.

The message replayed in her mind in pieces, she hears you, she's proud of you, she's with you and the girls, always.

Marie pressed her palm to her chest, right over her heart. The ache was still there, it always would be, but it felt different now, less sharp, less lonely.

She walked to the patio door and slid it open. The air outside was warm, the kind of Florida afternoon that wrapped around her like a soft blanket. She stepped out, Tyson following, and sat in her usual chair.

She didn't light a cigarette. She didn't need to. She just sat there, letting the air settle around her, letting the moment settle inside her.

A memory rose, not painful or heavy, just present, her daughter laughing in the passenger seat, feet on the dashboard, hair blowing in the wind. Marie talking to her the way she still did now, even when the seat was empty.

She smiled, a small, real smile. For the first time in a long time, the memory didn't hurt. It warmed her.

Marie took one more breath, slow and steady, and stood. She wasn't fixed, and she wasn't healed, but something inside her had shifted anyway, gently, quietly, undeniably. She carried that shift with her as she stepped back into the house.

She moved through the rest of the afternoon with a softness she hadn't felt in years, letting the moment settle inside her like warm water filling the cracks she had learned to ignore. Every so often, she touched her chest, right where the ache had softened, just to remind herself it was real.

By evening, she knew exactly who she needed to call.

Laura.

Her cousin, her mirror, the one who understood her heart without needing explanations. Laura had been born late in life to Marie's Aunt Carmella, a surprise baby, a blessing, a spark. She was only two years younger than Marie's daughter, and the girls had grown up side by side. Over the years, as life shifted and grief reshaped their families, Marie and Laura had become something deeper, two women who carried more than they ever said out loud.

Marie wiped her face, steadied her breath, and tapped Laura's name.

The phone rang twice.

"Hey," Laura answered, her voice warm, familiar, grounding. "I was just thinking about you."

Marie closed her eyes. "I… I need to tell you something."

Laura didn't rush her. She never did. "Okay. I'm here."

Marie took a breath that trembled on the way out. "It happened," she said softly. "I wasn't looking for anything. I wasn't even thinking about her. I was just scrolling, and this live came up."

Laura inhaled sharply but stayed quiet, letting Marie speak.

"It was a medium," Marie continued. "A woman. And she said she had a daughter with her. I almost scrolled past it, but… I didn't."

Her voice cracked, just once.

"She said the mom talks to her daughter in the car," Marie whispered. "Like she's sitting right there."

Laura exhaled, long and slow. "Oh, Marie…"

"And then she said she was a mother too. And she showed her the number three." Marie pressed her hand to her forehead. "Three girls. My girls."

Laura didn't speak. Marie could hear her breathing, steady and present.

"She described them," Marie said, her voice breaking again. "All three. Exactly. And she said… she said my daughter hears me. When I talk to her. When I ask her things."

A small sound escaped Laura, part gasp, part sob, part prayer.

Marie swallowed hard. "She said she's proud of me. That she's with me and the girls. Always."

There was a long silence on the other end, not empty but full, full of love, full of belief, full of the kind of understanding only Laura could offer.

When Laura finally spoke, her voice was thick with emotion. "Marie… that was her. That was Nina. I know it."

Marie pressed her fingers to her eyes, tears slipping through again. "I didn't expect it," she whispered. "I wasn't even thinking about her. It just... found me."

"That's how it works," Laura said softly. "Spirit doesn't come when we're searching. They come when our heart is open enough to hear them."

Marie let out a shaky breath. "It felt real."

"It was real," Laura said firmly. "She's with you. She always has been. And she knew you needed that today."

Marie didn't answer right away. She couldn't. Her throat was too tight, her heart too full.

Laura continued, her voice gentle but certain. "You're not imagining this. You're not reaching. This was a message. A gift. And you deserve it."

Marie closed her eyes, letting the truth of those words settle into the same place the medium's message had landed earlier, deep and warm and steady.

"Thank you," she whispered.

"You don't have to thank me," Laura said. "Just... let yourself believe it."

Marie nodded, even though Laura couldn't see her. For the first time in a long time, she did.

Chapter 36
Between Doubt and Hope

The next morning arrived the way mornings always did, quietly and without ceremony. Coffee brewed in the kitchen. The dogs waited to go out. The house stretched itself awake one room at a time, still heavy with sleep and routine.

Marie moved through it on instinct. She let Tyson outside first, then filled the Duchess's bowl, wiped the counter without really noticing she was doing it, and reached for her mug before the coffee had even finished dripping. These were motions she could perform half asleep, half thinking, half somewhere else entirely.

And this morning, part of her was somewhere else.

A voice lingered in her mind, soft and careful, she hears you in the car. Marie had woken up with those words still sitting in her chest, not loud, just present. They hadn't faded with sleep. They hadn't softened with daylight. They had followed her into the kitchen, into the quiet hum of another ordinary day.

She tried not thinking about it. She tried to focus on the girls' schedules, on the permission slip that still hadn't been signed. Life required her attention, and had never waited patiently for her emotions before. Still, her thoughts drifted back to the woman on the screen, to the way her voice had changed when Marie typed those words into the chat, to the way she had spoken Nina's love so clearly it had felt impossible.

Marie wrapped both hands around her mug and leaned against the counter, staring out the window at the pale morning light spreading across the backyard. Tyson trotted back inside and settled near her feet, sighing heavily as if the day already felt long.

"Don't start," Marie murmured to herself.

She had learned a long time ago not to build her heart on things she couldn't hold, not on promises, not on possibilities, not on moments that could disappear as quickly as they came. Hope was beautiful, but it could also be dangerous when you had already lost as much as she had.

She took a slow sip of coffee. Maybe it was coincidence. Maybe the woman said things like that to everyone. Maybe grief had filled in the blanks. Her practical side lined up its arguments neatly, the way it always did, but another part of her, quieter and harder to silence, whispered back that maybe it wasn't.

She finished wiping down the counter, moving through her tasks with the same steady rhythm she always carried. When Frances shuffled in, hair still messy and eyes half closed, Marie smiled and handed her a plate without being asked. When Lynn appeared next, already talking about her seedlings, Marie listened and nodded and reminded her she needed to log in for her online schooling.

On the outside, nothing had changed. On the inside, something had shifted just enough to be felt.

That night, after the girls were asleep and the house had settled into its familiar hush, Marie sat on the edge of her bed with Tyson curled at her feet. The window was cracked just enough to let in the soft sounds of the neighborhood settling for the night.

She held her phone in her hands for a moment, then set it face down on the nightstand. She didn't need to replay anything. She didn't need proof. What she had felt that afternoon was still there, steady and warm in her chest, like a small flame that hadn't gone out.

She lay back against her pillows and stared at the ceiling, thinking of Nina's laugh, of her voice, of the way she used to fill every room she entered. For once, the memories didn't crash into her. They drifted in gently, like something being returned instead of taken away.

"I heard you," she whispered into the quiet.

She didn't know who might hear it. She just knew she needed to say it.

Tyson shifted closer, his body solid and familiar against her leg. Marie rested her hand on his back, feeling the slow rise and fall of his breathing.

Tomorrow would come. It always did. There would be laundry to do, schedules to manage, worries to carry. But tonight, she let herself hold onto one simple truth, she was still loved, she was still guided, she was still walking forward even when the path felt uncertain.

And for the first time in a long while, that felt like enough.

Chapter 37
What She Never Said

Marie had learned, over time, how to stay busy. It wasn't something she had planned. It happened gradually, shaped by responsibility and grief and long years of being needed more than she was noticed. Somewhere along the way, she realized that as long as her hands were full, her mind stayed quieter. As long as she was doing something, she didn't have to sit with everything she felt.

So that afternoon, when the house finally emptied and the noise of the day faded, she stood in the kitchen for a long moment without moving. The counters were clean. The laundry was done. The small list in her head had been checked off. There was nothing left that required her immediate attention, and suddenly she didn't know what to do with herself.

She carried her coffee into the living room and sat on the couch, setting the mug on the table without turning on the television. Tyson lay nearby, lifting his head slightly whenever she shifted. Outside, the light softened as the sun lowered, casting long shadows across the yard in a way that always made her feel thoughtful.

She leaned back and closed her eyes.

At first, her thoughts stayed shallow, groceries, appointments, a message she still needed to return, the familiar mental loop that usually kept her grounded. But without anything to distract her, her mind drifted deeper, toward places she didn't often visit on purpose.

She thought about her mother, not in quick flashes or half formed memories, but clearly. She remembered her voice, especially the tone she used when giving advice she knew Marie might ignore. She remembered the way she sat at the kitchen table in the evenings, hands wrapped around a cup of tea, watching the rest of the family move around her with quiet affection.

Then she thought about Nina, not only about the illness or the hospital or the end. She remembered her as a teenager, sprawled across her bed, talking about things that seemed unimportant and somehow meant everything. She remembered her loud laugh in public places, the way she never apologized for taking up space, the way she would call three times in a row if Marie didn't answer.

For years, Marie had held those memories carefully, as if they might shatter if she pressed too hard. Lately, they were changing. They still hurt, but there was warmth in them now, too, something gentler than before.

She rested her head against the back of the couch and let herself stay with those thoughts, with everything, with the truth she rarely admitted, even to herself, that she had never really leaned on anyone, not fully, not in the way people were supposed to.

Even with Tom beside her, even with family checking in, even with friends offering help, she had always kept some part of herself guarded, some quiet place where fear and exhaustion lived alone. When her mother had been alive, that place had been smaller. She had leaned on her more than she realized at the time, more than she ever said out loud. After she was gone, Marie learned to hold herself up and everyone else at the same time.

It wasn't bravery. It was survival.

She opened her eyes and stared at the ceiling, following the faint shadows there. Somewhere down the street, a car door closed. A dog barked. Life continued, steady and unaware of everything she carried.

Her thoughts turned, as they often did lately, to the live video she had watched days earlier, to the words that had reached her when she hadn't been searching for anything, she hears you, she's proud of you, she's with you.

Marie still didn't know what she believed about that. She wasn't sure she ever would. But she knew what it had done to her. It had loosened something inside her, not enough to make her reckless with hope, but enough to let her breathe differently, enough to make her feel, for the first time in a long while, that maybe she didn't have to hold everything alone in quite the same way.

Tyson stood and came closer, resting his head against her leg. She reached down and rubbed behind his ears, grateful for the quiet comfort of something solid and uncomplicated.

"I'm tired," she murmured, mostly to herself, not tired of living, not tired of loving, just tired of carrying so much without ever setting it down.

She didn't cry, or fall apart. She simply allowed herself to feel what she usually packed away, the sadness, the gratitude, the anger, the love, the fear, all of it existing together without needing to be sorted.

When she finally stood, she felt different, not lighter, not healed, just more honest with herself. And for now, that was enough to feel like a beginning.

Chapter 38
Learning to Rest

Marie noticed it first in small ways. She started sitting down more, not because anyone told her to, and not because she suddenly had more time. There was still laundry to fold, appointments to remember, and a house that never truly stayed quiet for long. But her body had begun to insist on pauses she could no longer ignore, and for once, she listened.

Some afternoons, she would lower herself onto the couch with her coffee and let the laundry wait, not forever, just long enough to breathe and let her shoulders drop, long enough to feel the tension ease from her shoulders and neck.

Tom didn't comment. He rarely did. He moved through the house the way he always had, steady in his own routines and focused on his own world. They shared space, history, and responsibility, but emotional weight had never been something he carried easily. Marie had learned that early in their marriage, and over the years she had learned not to ask him to hold what he didn't know how to carry. She had made peace with that, for the most part.

The girls noticed.

"Grandma, you're sitting," Frances said one afternoon, half joking and half surprised as she passed through the living room with her backpack slung over one shoulder.

Marie smiled over the rim of her mug. "Don't get used to it."

But she stayed where she was.

Tyson lay stretched out at her feet, one paw resting against her slipper, his presence steady and familiar. The house hummed with its usual low rhythm, distant television noise, the dishwasher running, a phone vibrating somewhere in another room. It was the sound of life continuing, ordinary and unremarkable, and somehow comforting.

Marie leaned her head back against the cushion and closed her eyes for a moment.

For most of her life, she had believed rest had to be earned. You finished the list first. You solved the problem first. You carried everyone else first. Only then were you allowed to stop. She had believed that love meant exhaustion, that devotion meant depletion, that strength meant staying upright no matter how heavy things became. No one had taught her that. She had learned it slowly, through loss and crisis, through years of putting herself last without even realizing she was doing it.

Somewhere along the way, she had begun to understand something different. Stopping did not mean failing. Sitting did not mean quitting. Breathing did not mean giving up. It meant surviving with intention.

Lynn wandered in next, already talking about her plants and whether the weather would be right for transplanting later in the week. Marie listened, nodded, asked questions, and reminded her about her online lessons. Brooke followed soon after, complaining about traffic, deadlines, and being tired in that half joking, half serious way that made Marie smile.

She absorbed it all the way she always had, but now she didn't disappear inside it. She stayed herself.

Later that evening, after the house had settled and the girls had drifted into their rooms, Marie stood at the kitchen sink rinsing out her mug. Tom watched television in the other room. The dogs shifted and sighed in their sleep. Outside, the porch light glowed softly against the dark.

She dried her hands and leaned against the counter for a moment, letting the quiet settle around her.

She wasn't suddenly healed. She still woke up tired. She still worried too much. She still carried things she didn't talk about. But she was no longer drowning under them.

She had learned how to set some of them down, how to place them gently on the edge of her life instead of stacking them on her chest. She had learned that she could love fiercely without destroying herself in the process.

That night, as she turned off the lights and made her way down the hallway, Tyson rose and followed her as he always did. She paused at her bedroom door and looked back once, taking in the quiet house, the soft breathing, the familiar safety she had worked so hard to build.

She hadn't done it perfectly. She had done it faithfully. And that, she realized, had been enough.

Chapter 39
The Day She Moved Differently

Sunday mornings had always carried their own rhythm in the house, a slower kind of waking, a softer kind of light. Marie opened her eyes before the alarm, not because she had to, but because the quiet felt gentle enough to meet without rushing. She stayed still for a moment, letting the morning settle around her. Tyson lifted his head from the floor and watched her with calm, steady eyes, as if he sensed the shift before she did.

She sat up slowly, stretching her legs over the side of the bed. There was no list running through her mind yet, no urgency pushing her forward. She stood, walked to the kitchen, and started the coffee without multitasking. Tyson followed her, his nails tapping lightly against the floor, his presence familiar and grounding.

The house was still. The girls were asleep. Tom was snoring softly in the bedroom. Outside, the early light touched the tops of the trees, turning them a muted gold. Marie poured her coffee and stepped onto the patio, letting the warm air wrap around her. She sat in her usual chair and took a slow sip, feeling the quiet settle inside her instead of pressing against her.

She did not reach for her phone. She did not think about the laundry. She did not plan the day before it arrived. She simply breathed.

By the time she heard movement inside, she felt more awake than she had in days.

Frances shuffled into the kitchen first, hair messy, eyes half closed. She blinked at Marie through the sliding glass door.

"You're outside early," she said, stepping onto the patio.

Marie smiled. "Just enjoying the morning."

Frances nodded, still waking up, and leaned against the doorframe. "Dad and Ann said they're coming around ten."

"I know," Marie said. "We'll be ready."

Frances went back inside, and Marie stayed where she was, letting the moment linger. She felt the difference in herself, not dramatic, not loud, just present. A small shift, but real.

By midmorning, the house was awake. Lynn talked about her plants while she watered the ones on the porch. Brooke came out of her apartment complaining about being tired, her voice half joking and half serious. It wasn't like her to be up this early. Tom moved through the kitchen in his usual quiet way, making himself a sandwich even though it was barely ten o'clock.

Marie moved among them without rushing, she did not hover. She listened, but she did not absorb everything the way she used to. She let the girls talk without feeling the need to fix anything. She let the morning unfold without trying to control it.

When William's truck pulled into the driveway, Tyson began to bark. Marie opened the sliding glass door just as William and Ann stepped onto the porch. William looked tired, but lighter than he had in months. Ann smiled warmly, her presence gentle and steady.

"Morning," William said, leaning in to hug her.

"Morning," Marie replied, hugging him back.

Ann stepped forward next, wrapping Marie in a soft, sincere embrace. "You look good today," she said quietly.

Marie felt the words land somewhere deep. "Thank you," she said, and she meant it.

The girls came rushing in behind her, pulling William and Ann into the house with their usual mix of excitement and teasing. The living room filled quickly with voices, laughter, and the easy chaos of family. Marie stood back for a moment, watching them all, feeling something inside her settle in a way she had not expected.

She joined them on the couch, Tyson settling at her feet. She listened to William talk about work, to Ann talk about a recipe she wanted to try, to the girls argue playfully about who was going to make dinner. She felt present, not pulled in a dozen directions, not bracing for the next thing.

Just present.

Later, when the house quieted again and William and Ann said their goodbyes, Marie walked them to the door. William hugged her a second time, holding on a little longer than usual.

"You doing okay?" he asked softly.

Marie nodded. "I think so."

He searched her face for a moment, then nodded back. "Good."

After they left, Marie stood in the doorway for a moment, letting the warm air brush against her skin. She felt the shift again, small but steady, like something inside her had loosened just enough to let the day in without resistance.

She closed the door and leaned against it, breathing in the quiet.

She was not healed. She was not finished. But she was moving differently, softer, slower, more aware of herself than she had been in a long time.

And for the first time, she let herself believe that maybe this was what beginning again looked like.

Chapter 40
When Someone Finally Noticed

Monday morning settled over the house in its usual slow way, but Marie felt steadier as she moved through the kitchen. She poured her coffee, slid open the patio door, and stepped outside with her cigarette already between her fingers. The air was cool and soft against her skin, and she let herself sink into her chair without thinking about the dishes in the sink or the day waiting for her. Tyson followed her out and settled at her feet, watching her with the same quiet certainty he had the day before, as if he knew she was still carrying that small shift inside her.

She took a long sip of coffee and let the morning settle around her. The yard was still, the sky pale, the world not quite awake yet. She breathed in the quiet and felt it settle in her chest instead of pressing against her. She didn't reach for her phone. She didn't think about the laundry, or plan the day before it arrived. She simply sat, letting the moment be what it was.

Inside, she heard the familiar sounds of the house waking. A door closing. Footsteps. The soft clatter of someone opening a cabinet. Tom shuffled into the kitchen, moving slowly the way he always did in the mornings. He glanced out the window and saw her on the patio, but he didn't interrupt. He poured himself a cup of coffee and wandered to the table, leaving her in the quiet she had chosen.

A few minutes passed before the sliding door opened again. Tom stepped outside, holding his mug in both hands. He didn't sit, just stood there for a moment, looking at her the way he sometimes did when he wasn't sure what to say.

"You're quiet today," he said softly.

Marie looked up at him, surprised by the gentleness in his voice. "Just enjoying the morning."

Tom nodded, studying her for a second longer than usual. "You look… good," he said, the words simple but sincere. Then he took a sip of his coffee and went back inside, leaving the door cracked behind him.

Marie watched him go, feeling the words settle somewhere deep. Tom didn't comment on much. He didn't always know how to carry the emotional weight of the house, but when he noticed something, it meant he truly saw it.

A little while later, her phone buzzed on the table beside her. She picked it up and saw a message from Ann.

You seemed really peaceful yesterday. I hope today feels the same.

Marie stared at the screen for a moment, her chest warming in a way she hadn't expected. She typed back a simple thank you, then set the phone down again. She didn't need to say more. The acknowledgment alone felt like enough.

Later, when the house grew louder and the day began to take shape, Marie moved through it with the same steady calm she had carried onto the patio. She wiped the counter, but she didn't hover. She listened to Frances chattering on the phone while she got ready for school, but she didn't absorb everything the way she used to. She let the day unfold without trying to control it.

By the afternoon, she found herself back on the patio with a fresh cup of coffee, Tyson curled at her feet. She thought about the small moments from the morning, the message from Ann, and the way Tom had paused in the doorway, really looking at her. She realized she had been seen in a way she wasn't used to, not for what she carried, but for how she was beginning to set some of it down.

She leaned back in her chair and let the quiet settle around her again.

She was not healed. She was not finished. But she was moving differently, softer, slower, more aware of herself than she had been in a long time.

And for the first time, she let herself believe that maybe others could see it too

Chapter 41
The Truth She Shared

Marie had been carrying the news quietly for weeks, tucked into the same place she kept all the things she didn't want to burden anyone with. The doctor had been gentle when he told her, explaining the numbers, the risks, the next steps. She had nodded, asked the right questions, and walked out of the office with a prescription for insulin folded neatly in her purse. She had driven home in silence, letting the weight of it settle beside her like an unwelcome passenger.

She hadn't told the girls. She hadn't told Tom. She hadn't told anyone. She didn't want to see worry in their faces or hear the panic in their voices. She didn't want to be the reason anyone felt afraid. So, she learned the routine quietly, checking her sugar, adjusting her meals, giving herself the injections with a steady hand even on the days she didn't feel steady at all.

But that afternoon, something in her felt different. She had spent the morning moving through the house with the same calm she had carried from the day before, letting the quiet settle around her instead of fighting it. She sat on the patio with her coffee, Tyson curled at her feet, the warm air brushing against her skin. She felt the shift inside her, small but steady, and she knew she couldn't keep everything tucked away forever.

Her phone rang on the table beside her. She glanced at the screen and saw her brother's name. She hesitated for a moment, then answered.

"Hey," she said, her voice soft.

"Hey," he replied. "Just checking in. How's your day going?"

Marie looked out at the yard, the sunlight catching on the leaves. "It's been quiet," she said. "Good, actually."

"That's nice," he said. "You sound better than you have in a while."

She smiled faintly. "I feel a little better."

There was a pause, the kind that only existed between people who didn't need to fill silence to feel close. Marie took a slow breath, feeling the familiar tightness in her chest, the one that came whenever she thought about the things she kept hidden.

"There's something I should tell you," She said quietly.

Anthony didn't rush her. "Okay."

Marie stared at the steam rising from her coffee. "When I went to the doctor a few weeks ago… he put me on insulin."

There was a soft inhale on the other end of the line, not sharp, not panicked, just surprised. "Marie," he said gently. "Why didn't you tell me?"

"I didn't want to worry anyone," she said. "I didn't want the girls to panic. I didn't want Tom to make a big deal out of it. I just… handled it."

Anthony was quiet for a moment, and when he spoke again, his voice was steady. "You don't have to handle everything alone."

"I know," she whispered, though she wasn't sure she fully believed it.

"You should have told me, He said, not with anger, but with understanding. "Not because I'd worry, but because I get it. I know what it feels like. I know the routine. I know the fear. You don't have to pretend with me."

Marie felt her throat tighten. She blinked hard, staring at the yard until the shapes blurred. "I didn't want to be a burden."

"You're not," he said firmly. "You never have been."

She let the words settle, warm and unfamiliar. Tyson shifted closer, resting his head against her leg as if he sensed the heaviness in her chest.

"How are you feeling with it?" Anthony asked.

"Okay," she said. "Better now that I said it out loud."

"That's how it works," he said. "You carry it alone until you don't have too anymore."

Marie nodded, even though he couldn't see her. "Thank you," she said softly.

"You don't have to thank me," he replied. "Just promise me you'll tell me next time. You don't have to hide things from me."

"I won't," she said, and for the first time, she meant it.

They talked a little longer, about ordinary things, about the girls, about the weather, about nothing important and everything that mattered. When she hung up, Marie sat back in her chair and let the quiet settle around her again.

She felt lighter, not because the burden was gone, but because she had finally shared it. She had let someone in. She had allowed herself to be understood.

She looked out at the yard, the sunlight shifting across the grass, and felt something inside her loosen just a little more.

She leaned back in her chair, surprised by the calm settling through her. She hadn't expected sharing the truth to feel like this. She hadn't expected it to feel like relief.

Chapter 42
A Familiar Echo

Marie stood at the kitchen table, folding a small pile of laundry she had pulled from the dryer. The house was quiet in that late-afternoon way, the kind of quiet that came after the girls had settled into their routines and Tom had wandered off to watch something on the living room TV. Tyson lay stretched out near the sliding door, his tail thumping lazily every now and then as he drifted in and out of sleep.

She folded a towel, smoothing the edges with her palms, and reached for the next one. As she lifted it, a faint smell drifted from the kitchen behind her, something warm and familiar. She had left a pot simmering on the stove, nothing special, just a simple sauce for dinner. But the scent rising from it, tomatoes, garlic, a hint of basil, caught her in a way she hadn't expected.

It was the smell of her mother's kitchen.

Not the exact recipe, not the exact moment, but the feeling of it. The way her mother used to hum while stirring a pot, the soft clatter of a wooden spoon against the side of a pan, the warmth that filled the house on days when everything felt too heavy. Marie paused, towel in her hands, letting the memory wash over her. It didn't knock the air out of her the way it once would have. It didn't send her spiraling or make her chest tighten with panic. It simply arrived, soft and familiar, like a visitor she hadn't seen in a while.

She closed her eyes for a moment, breathing in the scent, letting it settle. She could almost hear her mother's voice, low and steady, telling her to taste the sauce, to add a little more salt, to slow down and let things simmer. The ache was there, but it wasn't sharp. It was warm, almost comforting.

The sliding door opened behind her, and Brooke stepped in from her apartment, her hair pulled up in a messy bun, her phone in her hand. She stopped when she saw Marie standing still, towel half folded, eyes distant.

"You okay?" Brooke asked, her voice gentle.

Marie blinked and looked over at her granddaughter. "Yeah," she said softly. "Just thinking."

Brooke stepped closer, sniffing the air. "Smells like Grandma's sauce," she said, smiling a little. "I haven't thought about that in a long time."

Marie felt something loosen in her chest. "Me neither," she said. "It just… hit me."

Brooke nodded, leaning against the counter. "It's a good smell," she said. "A good memory."

Marie returned the smile, small but real. "Yeah," she said. "It is."

Brooke stayed for a moment, scrolling through her phone, talking about something she had seen online, something light and easy. Marie listened, letting the sound of her granddaughter's voice pull her fully back into the present. The memory didn't disappear, but it settled into place, no longer overwhelming, no longer something she had to push away.

When Brooke headed back to her apartment, Marie finished folding the laundry, placing each piece into neat stacks. She moved slowly, aware of the quiet shift inside her. The past had brushed against her, but it hadn't swallowed her. She had held it, felt it, and stayed steady.

She carried the folded clothes to the bedroom, then stepped outside onto the patio with her coffee, letting the warm air wrap around her. The yard was calm, the evening light softening the edges of everything it touched. She sat down, feeling the weight of the day settle in a way that felt gentle rather than heavy.

She looked out at the yard, thinking of her mother, thinking of the smell from the kitchen, thinking of Brooke's smile. She felt the past and the present sitting side by side inside her, no longer fighting for space.

"I'm learning to live with both the past and the present," she thought, the words settling into her like truth.

She took a slow sip of her coffee and let the quiet hold her..

Chapter 43
When She Joined In

The house was warm with the sound of the girls' laughter long before Marie realized what they were doing. She had been in the kitchen, rinsing a few dishes and wiping down the counter, moving slowly through the familiar motions of the evening. Tyson paced around her feet, hopeful for crumbs, his tail brushing against her leg every few steps. She could hear the girls talking over one another, their voices rising and falling in that playful way that always meant they were up to something.

When she stepped into the living room, she saw all three of them gathered around the coffee table, a Monopoly board spread out between them. Money was scattered everywhere, tokens lined up in uneven rows, and Brooke was leaning forward with her elbows on her knees, arguing about rent with Frances while Lynn counted her bills with exaggerated seriousness.

Brooke looked up first. "Grandma," she said, smiling. "Come sit with us."

Marie paused, her hand still resting on the back of the couch. For a moment, she felt the familiar instinct to stay on the edges, to watch from a distance, to let them have their fun without her. But the hesitation passed quickly, softer than it used to be. She didn't overthink it. She didn't talk herself out of it. She simply walked around the couch and sat down beside Brooke.

Brooke nudged her shoulder gently. "Good. Now you can help me bankrupt your other two grandchildren."

Frances gasped dramatically. "She's not helping you. She's on my team."

Lynn rolled her eyes. "Grandma is neutral. She's Switzerland."

Marie laughed, the sound surprising her with how easily it came. She picked up a stray piece of Monopoly money and smoothed it between her fingers, watching the girls bicker and tease each other. Tyson settled at her feet, letting out a long sigh as if he approved of her choice to join them.

The girls kept playing, arguing over rules they all pretended to know, accusing each other of cheating, celebrating every small victory. Marie found herself laughing at their jokes, shaking her head at their antics, leaning into the moment without feeling the usual pull back into her thoughts. She wasn't drifting. She wasn't stuck in her head.

She was here.

With them.

Present in a way she hadn't been in a long time.

At one point, Brooke made a ridiculous face at Frances, who burst into laughter so loud it startled Tyson. Marie laughed too, her hand covering her mouth, her eyes watering from the sudden joy of it. It felt good. It felt real. It felt like something she had been missing without even realizing it.

They played until the game fell apart the way Monopoly always did, with someone quitting, someone claiming victory, and someone insisting the rules had been wrong the entire time. The girls drifted off to their rooms, still talking, still laughing, leaving the board half-packed on the table.

Marie stood and stretched, feeling the warmth of the evening settle into her bones. She walked to the sliding door and stepped outside, the night air cool against her skin. The yard was quiet, the sky darkening into a soft blue, and the world felt steady in a way she hadn't felt in a long time.

She leaned back in her chair, breathing in the calm. She wasn't thinking about yesterday or tomorrow. She wasn't replaying old memories or bracing for new ones. She wasn't stuck in her head.

She was simply here, in this moment, part of her own life again.

Chapter 44
What She Picked Up Again

The morning moved quietly through the house, sunlight stretching across the floor in long, warm lines. Marie finished her coffee on the patio, letting the calm settle into her the way it had been doing more often lately. Tyson lay beside her chair, his head resting on her foot, content with the slow start to the day. When she finally stepped back inside, the house felt still in a comforting way, not empty, just peaceful.

She walked through the living room, picking up a blanket someone had left on the couch, straightening a pillow, moving without hurry. As she passed the small table near the hallway, something caught her eye. Her sketchbook sat there, half tucked beneath a stack of mail, the corner of its worn cover peeking out as if it had been waiting for her.

She paused, her hand hovering over it. She hadn't touched it in years. Not because she didn't want to, but because life had filled every corner of her days, leaving no room for the quiet things she once loved.

She stared at it for a moment, a familiar ache rising in her chest, not sadness exactly, but recognition.

She didn't overthink it.

She just… picked it up.

The cover felt soft from years of use, the pages inside slightly warped from time and humidity. She carried it to the kitchen table and sat down, flipping it open to a blank page. The pencil she kept tucked in the binding rolled into her hand as if it belonged there.

She didn't try to draw anything specific. She didn't plan a scene or a face or a memory. She simply let the pencil touch the page and sketched a single line, then another, letting her hand move without expectation. The lines were simple, soft, almost hesitant, but they felt right. They felt like hers.

The house was quiet except for the soft scratch of graphite on paper. Tyson wandered over and lay at her feet again, his presence grounding her. She kept drawing, letting the lines build into something gentle and familiar, something she didn't need to name yet.

A few minutes passed before she heard footsteps behind her. Lynn walked into the kitchen, her hair still messy from sleep, her tablet tucked under her arm. She stopped when she saw Marie at the table, her eyes widening just a little.

Without saying anything, Lynn pulled out the chair beside her and sat down. She didn't ask what Marie was drawing. She didn't comment on the sketchbook or the lines on the page. She simply sat there, quiet and steady, the way she always did when she sensed something delicate unfolding.

Marie kept sketching, her movements slow and easy. She didn't feel self-conscious. She didn't feel the need to explain herself. Lynn's quiet presence felt natural, comforting, like a soft weight settling beside her.

After a while, Lynn leaned her head against Marie's shoulder, just for a moment, then sat back up and opened her tablet. She didn't say a word, but she didn't need to. Her being there was enough.

Marie finished the last line of her sketch and set the pencil down, looking at the page without judgment. It wasn't perfect. It wasn't meant to be. It was simply hers, a small piece of herself she hadn't touched in far too long.

She closed the sketchbook gently and stood, feeling something warm settle inside her. She walked to the sliding door and stepped outside, the air soft against her skin. The yard was quiet, morning light shifting across the grass, and she felt connected to herself in a way she hadn't in years.

She breathed in slowly, letting the moment settle.

She wasn't trying to become someone new.

She was remembering someone she had always been.

And that felt like coming home.

Chapter 45
When the Distance Softened

The house settled into its evening hum, each girl tucked into her own little world. Brooke was in her apartment, music drifting faintly through the shared wall as she cleaned or rearranged something, the way she always did when she needed to reset her mind. Frances was on the phone in her room, her voice rising and falling in animated bursts as she paced across the floor. Lynn sat curled in the recliner, her tablet propped on her knees, playing a game she had downloaded.

Marie sat on the other end of the couch with Tyson pressed against her hip, his head resting on her thigh. She stroked the soft fur behind his ears, letting the steady rhythm of the house settle around her. It was the kind of evening that didn't ask anything of her, warm and familiar without being loud or overwhelming.

She didn't hear Tom come in at first. He moved quietly, the way he often did when the girls were occupied and the house felt peaceful. He walked through the kitchen, grabbed a drink from the fridge, and paused in the doorway to the living room. For a moment he just watched them. Lynn absorbed in her screen. Tyson snoring softly. Marie sitting with her shoulders relaxed in a way he hadn't seen in a long time. He crossed the room and sat beside her, not too close, not too far, just enough that she could feel the warmth of him. He didn't say anything. He didn't ask anything. He simply settled in, letting the quiet fill the space between them.

A few minutes passed before he reached for the blanket draped over the back of the couch. He unfolded it slowly and laid it across her legs with a gentleness that surprised her. It wasn't a grand gesture. It wasn't an apology or a question. It was simply care, quiet, steady, familiar.

Marie looked down at the blanket, then at him. He didn't meet her eyes, just leaned back and took a slow sip of his drink, his gaze drifting toward the TV Marie was half watching. She waited for the old irritation to rise, the instinct to pull away or retreat into her thoughts. But it didn't come. Instead, she felt something settle inside her, something calm and steady.

She let the blanket rest where he placed it.

Tyson shifted, pressing closer to her side. Marie glanced down with a small smile before looking back at the TV. The room felt warm in a way she hadn't noticed in a long time, not heavy, not tense, just lived-in and soft.

Tom let out a quiet sigh, the kind he made when he finally relaxed after a long day. Marie felt the sound more than she heard it, a small vibration in the cushion between them. She didn't move away. She didn't overthink it. She simply stayed where she was, letting the moment be what it was.

The distance between them didn't disappear. It didn't need to. It just softened, enough for her to breathe without feeling like she was bracing for something. Enough for him to sit beside her without feeling like he was intruding.

When the girls drifted off to their rooms and the house grew quiet again, Marie stood and walked to the sliding door. She stepped outside, the night air cool against her skin, and looked out across the yard. The sky was darkening, the last traces of daylight fading into soft blue.

For the first time that day, she felt steady, not overwhelmed, not guarded.

Just steady.

She didn't know what the moment on the couch meant, not yet. But she knew it didn't feel heavy. It didn't feel like pressure or expectation. It felt simple. It felt human. It felt like something she could let herself lean into, slowly, gently, in her own time.

And for now, simple was enough.

Chapter 46
The Quiet She Noticed

The house was unusually still, the kind that only happened when everyone else was sleeping in. Brooke was tucked away in her apartment, Frances hadn't stirred yet, and Lynn's door remained closed. Even Tom was outside somewhere, the faint sound of him moving around the yard drifting in through the cracked door. Tyson lay stretched out on the floor, his body long and relaxed, his breathing slow and steady.

Marie stood in the kitchen for a moment, taking in the silence. It wasn't the heavy kind she used to dread, the kind that made her chest tighten. This was different. This was gentle. She moved slowly, filling the coffee maker listening to the soft drip as it brewed. When it finished, she poured herself a cup and held it between her hands, letting the warmth settle into her palms.

She walked through the living room, noticing how the morning light fell across the floor in soft, pale stripes. She wasn't rushing, or bracing. She wasn't waiting for the next crisis to pull her out of herself. She simply moved, steady and unhurried, letting the quiet settle around her.

She lit a candle on the counter, the flame flickering to life with a soft glow. The scent drifted upward, warm and familiar, filling the room with something that felt like home. With her coffee in hand, she stepped onto the patio and sat down, the early air cool against her skin. Tyson lifted his head briefly, then settled again, content.

Marie took a slow sip of her coffee and let her eyes drift across the yard. The quiet felt different today. It wasn't empty. It wasn't lonely. It was peaceful in a way she hadn't felt in a long time.

Her thoughts drifted to the smell from the kitchen the other day, the one that had reminded her of her mother. She remembered how it had washed over her, not with pain, but with warmth. She thought about the sketch she had drawn, the simple line that had felt like a small return to herself. She thought about the moment with Tom on the couch, the blanket he had placed over her legs, the way she hadn't pulled away. All of it connected, small threads weaving together into something steady and quiet inside her.

She sat there for a long moment, letting the morning settle around her. She didn't feel the familiar weight pressing on her chest. She didn't feel the fog she had been moving through for so long. She felt calm.

Just calm.

She breathed in the cool air, letting it fill her slowly. She didn't know what the rest of the day would bring, but for the first time in a long time, she didn't feel like she had to prepare for anything. She didn't feel like she had to hold herself together. She simply felt present.

She closed her eyes for a moment, letting the quiet hold her, and when she opened them again, the world felt a little softer.

She felt steady, she felt like herself.

Chapter 47
A Day That Felt Like a Beginning

The house woke with a soft, familiar hum, the kind that meant everyone was easing into the day at their own pace. Brooke came in from her apartment with her hair pulled up and a tote bag slung over her shoulder, the kind she always took to the oddities markets. Frances wandered into the kitchen, scrolling through her phone, already laughing at something she hadn't explained yet. Lynn was in her room with her tablet, tapping through a game.

Marie moved through the kitchen with a quiet steadiness, rinsing a cup, wiping the counter, listening to the gentle sound of the house. It reminded her of the mornings she used to have before everything became complicated, the soft rise of voices, the clatter of dishes, the hum of people waking up. It reminded her, too, of the mornings she used to talk to her aunt on the phone, their conversations weaving into the start of her day like a familiar thread.

She wasn't waiting for the next crisis or bracing for one. She was simply here.

Brooke dropped her tote bag onto the counter with a thud. "Grandma," she said, pulling something wrapped in brown paper from inside, "I need your opinion on this. And don't freak out."

Marie raised an eyebrow but didn't react. "All right," she said, steady and calm.

Brooke unwrapped the paper, revealing a glass jar filled with clear preserving fluid. Inside, coiled neatly, was a large snake, delicate and suspended as if frozen mid-movement.

Marie blinked once. "Oh," she said softly. "That's… something."

Brooke grinned. "Right? Isn't it cool?"

Marie leaned in a little, studying it without flinching. She didn't love it, but she wasn't rattled either. It was Brooke, of course she'd come home with something like this. "It's definitely unique," she said. "Where are you thinking of putting it?"

Brooke lit up. "I knew you'd get it. I was thinking my shelf, next to the other animals."

Marie nodded. "That works."

Brooke carried the wrapped jar back toward her apartment, still talking about where she might put it. Frances wandered off to show Lynn something on her phone, their voices overlapping in the easy way they always did.

Marie stayed in the kitchen for a moment, wiping her hands on a towel, listening to the soft rise of voices around her. The house felt awake, not chaotic, just full in a way she hadn't felt in a long time. She wasn't standing on the outside of it anymore. She was in it.

She moved to the sink, rinsed her cup. The simple motion felt steady and natural. She didn't feel the old tightness in her chest. She didn't feel like she was bracing for something to go wrong. She felt… here.

Frances poked her head back into the kitchen, still holding her phone. "Grandma, look at this," she said, already laughing before Marie even turned around. She crossed the room in a few quick steps and held out the screen, some ridiculous video playing: a cat wearing sunglasses, dancing terribly to a song Marie didn't recognize.

Marie couldn't help it. She laughed. Not a polite laugh, not a forced one, a real one, the kind that came from somewhere easy.

Frances leaned against her shoulder for a second, warm and familiar, then straightened up. "I knew you'd think it was funny," she said, grinning before darting back toward the hallway, calling for Lynn to watch it next.

Marie watched her go, the sound of her laughter drifting through the house. Tyson trotted after her, nails tapping across the floor, tail wagging like he was in on the joke.

The morning moved around Marie in soft pieces, voices overlapping, doors opening and closing, Brooke humming as she rearranged something in her apartment. And for the first time in a long time, Marie didn't feel like she was trying to catch up to the day.

She was part of it now.

Right in the middle of it.

Steady.

Chapter 48
A Call She Was Ready For

The afternoon settled into its usual rhythm. Lynn was in her room with her tablet, Tyson stretched across her feet like a warm, oversized cat. Frances was sprawled on the couch, laughing at something on her phone. Brooke was in her apartment rearranging her shelves again, probably finding the perfect spot for the snake in the jar.

Marie stood at the kitchen counter folding a small stack of towels, the kind of simple task that didn't demand anything from her. The house hummed around her.

Her phone buzzed on the counter.

She glanced at the screen and paused.

Ava.

Ava's voice always carried that bright, steady energy Marie had known for years, the kind that made her picture her step-sister moving through her day with a classroom full of kids on one side and a trail of grandchildren on the other. Even over the phone, Marie could hear the movement in her life, the boys calling in the background, a grandchild laughing, something clattering in the kitchen. Ava never stopped. She had a full schedule, a full heart, and somehow, she still made room for Marie.

Marie answered, and they slipped into conversation the way they always did, picking up threads that had been waiting for them.

They talked about the girls, about school, about the little things that filled their days. Ava told her a quick story about one of her students, and

Marie told her about Brooke's snake in the jar, which made Ava groan and laugh at the same time.

As they talked, Marie found herself thinking back to the last time they'd seen each other, Sophia's funeral. A sad day, but seeing all of Ava's boys together had reminded her how big that side of the family had become. And her nephew Michael… seeing him again had tugged at something soft in her. She used to watch him when he was little, back when everyone lived closer and life felt more connected. Now they were all scattered across states and time zones, and moments like that were rare.

They talked a little longer before Ava had to go, grandkids arriving, dinner to start, a life full of motion waiting for her. They promised to talk again soon, even though both of them knew "soon" might be weeks or months. It didn't matter. The connection was still there.

When the call ended, Marie set the phone down and stood for a moment, letting the feeling settle.

She felt… connected.

The house moved around her, Frances laughing in the living room, Lynn calling for Tyson, Tom fixing a broken toilet, and Marie stepped back into it without hesitation.

Her world felt a little bigger again.

Chapter 49
The Quiet She Finally Found

The house was quiet, but not the hollow quiet it used to be. Not the kind that pressed against her chest and reminded her of everything she had lost. This quiet was different. It was soft. It held life inside it.

Marie stood at the kitchen counter with a warm mug in her hands, watching the sunlight stretch across the floor. The refrigerator hummed. A ceiling fan turned slowly. Somewhere in the house, a door clicked shut. Normal sounds. Comforting ones. She took a slow sip of her coffee and leaned against the counter, letting herself stay in the moment.

For a long time, mornings had been something she simply endured. Something she pushed through. Wake up. Get moving. Don't think too much. Don't feel too deeply. Just survive. But this morning, she wasn't bracing herself. She wasn't waiting for bad news. She wasn't scanning the house for signs of trouble. She was simply here.

From the living room came Lynn's soft laughter, mixed with the sound of a video playing. Frances sat at the table, focused on her schoolwork, her pencil tapping lightly against the page. Tyson lay near the doorway, one eye open, always watching, always close. Marie's heart softened at the sight. So much had been taken from them. So much had changed. And yet, so much remained: love, routine, connection, life.

She carried her mug out onto the patio and settled into her familiar chair, the one she had sat in so many times before, through grief, through fear, through exhaustion, through prayer. This place had seen her at her weakest. Now it saw her steady.

Tom stepped outside a moment later. "Morning," he said.

"Morning," she replied.

He studied her for a second. "You okay?"

Once, that question had been hard. Once, she had said "I'm fine" when she wasn't. Once, she had swallowed the truth and kept going anyway. Now, she smiled.

"Yeah," she said softly. "I really am."

He nodded, satisfied, and went back inside.

Marie stayed where she was, watching the yard, listening to the sounds of her family moving through the house. Her mother's voice no longer floated through the house. Nina's laughter no longer filled the rooms. Some losses never stopped hurting. They simply became part of who you were. But love didn't disappear. It lived in memories, in habits, in the way she tucked the girls in at night, in the way she still talked to them in her heart, in the strength they had passed down to her without even knowing it.

She closed her eyes for a moment and breathed in. Not in pain. In gratitude. For the years. For the lessons. For the love. For the chance to still be here. To still be needed. To still grow.

When she opened her eyes, Lynn stood in the doorway, watching her.

"Whatcha doing?" she asked.

Marie smiled. "Just enjoying the quiet."

Lynn nodded, as if she understood, then went back inside.

Marie finished her coffee and stood, ready to begin the day. Not because she had to. Because she wanted to.

The house was quiet.

And for the first time in a long time, it felt like home.

Six months later…

Marie sits on the patio with coffee.

The girls laugh inside.

Life isn't perfect.

But the light stayed on.